CALEB'S CAB

Story by

Sally Chomet

Illustrated by

Sylvain Chomet

WALKER
BOOKS

First published in Great Britain 2016 by Walker Books Ltd
87 Vauxhall Walk, London SE11 5HJ

This edition published in 2017

2 4 6 8 10 9 7 5 3 1

Text © 2016 Sally Chomet
Illustrations © 2016 Sylvain Chomet

The right of Sally Chomet and Sylvain Chomet to be identified as
author and illustrator respectivly of this work has been asserted by them
in accordance with the Copyright, Designs and Patents Act 1988

This book has been typeset in Goudy

Printed and bound by CPI Group (UK) Ltd, Croydon CR0 4YY

British Library Cataloguing in Publication Data:
a catalogue record for this book is available from the British Library

ISBN 978-1-4063-4228-4
www.walker.co.uk

MIX
Paper from
responsible sources
FSC® C020471

CALEB'S CAB

For Jinty and Ludo

Chapter One

"What's *that?*" Mopsy whined as she peered over her son's shoulder.

"Spam curry," said Caleb proudly, spooning steaming pink cubes of meat and red sauce onto two plates.

Ever since his dad had gone missing, eleven-year-old Caleb did all the chores in the Dallaway household. His mother couldn't even make a cup of tea. The closest Mopsy came to cooking was concocting her natural-product face masks. She didn't have any cookbooks, so Caleb made up most of his recipes as he went along. They were rarely successful.

Mopsy pushed the chunks of spam slowly around her plate. She was sulking, her lips, thick with lipstick, sticking out in a pout. Caleb ate quickly and had just finished his last mouthful when the doorbell rang. "I'll get that," he said.

The two of them jumped up from their seats, Mopsy abandoning her untouched meal. While Caleb rushed to the front door, she began setting up a strange machine on the table. It looked a bit like an electric sandwich-maker with two smooth, jaw-like plates.

"Ah, good evening, Officer Lumley!" came Caleb's voice from the hallway. "Won't you come in? Mum, it's the police!" he called, leading the officer through the hall and into the dining room.

As they entered, a red light flicked to green on Mopsy's peculiar machine. Without looking up, she opened the lid and put her head inside, squashing her cheeks between the plates. The contraption hissed and steamed like an iron, sending odd-smelling vapours billowing out into the room. Caleb's own face reddened as he looked up at the policeman. "Would you like a cup of tea?" he offered.

"No, thank you. This is just a routine visit. There's been another possible sighting of your father."

Instantly Caleb's embarrassment was forgotten. "Where?" he asked excitedly. "How long ago?"

"A man matching Mr Dallaway's description was seen an

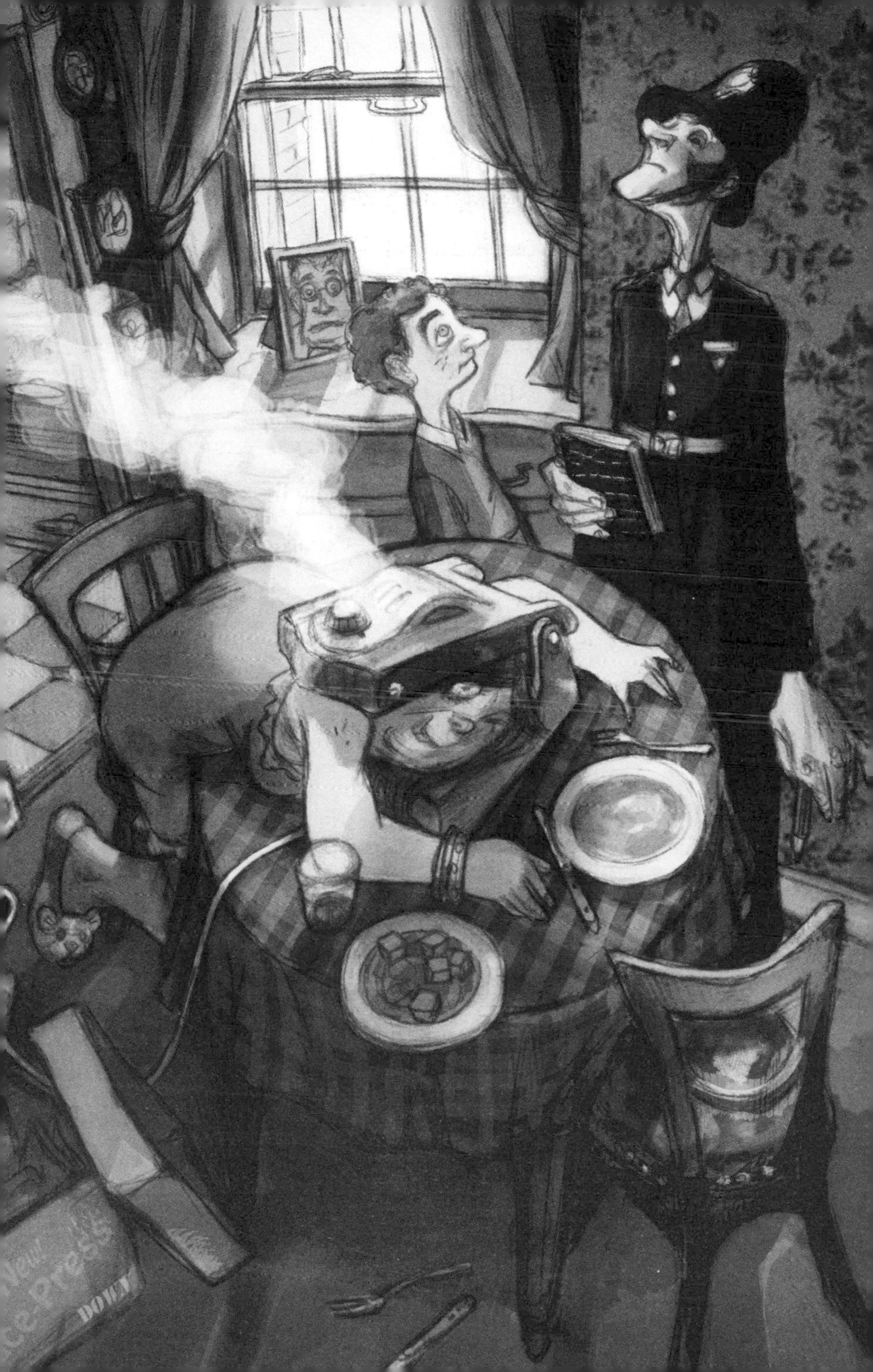
DOWN

hour ago outside The Red Lion pub," said Officer Lumley, glancing at Mopsy, who had disappeared in another puff of steam. "A member of the public phoned with the details..." He flipped open his notebook to read the name:

mr Will E.Turnup

Caleb raised his eyebrows. There had been many bogus sightings before this one.

"Of course, we will keep you informed if the lead turns out to be substantial," Lumley added.

Just then Mopsy's machine pinged like a microwave. She opened the lid and lifted out her head. Her skin was red and greasy. She picked up a hand mirror and gasped with delight.

"Mum, there's been another sighting of Dad!" said Caleb.

"Another hoax, I suppose?" said Mopsy, fluffing up her hair and returning to her reflection.

"The scene is being investigated as we speak, Mrs Dallaway," said the officer. "You must be encouraged that the case remains high profile. Your husband was – *is* – a highly respected member of the community."

"Yes, there aren't many like him left nowadays," Mopsy sighed.

The policeman nodded. "Leftwinger, cab driver, historian, devoted father and active library campaigner… Bert Dallaway was one of our last crusaders! Like you say – few of his kind…"

Mopsy interrupted. "Will that be all?"

"Yes, that's all for now," he said, snapping the notebook shut. "Have a good evening, Mrs Dallaway. We'll be in touch."

He showed himself out. Meanwhile Caleb wrote down the details of the possible sighting on a Post-it note. "I'm going to follow this up," he said, "before I start work..." He paused a moment. "What *is* that thing you were squashing your head in just now?"

"It's a *face-press*," Mopsy trilled. "I bought it today. Marvellous, don't you think?"

"*How* did you buy it? Have you borrowed more money from Mr Measles?"

Mopsy let the mirror drop. "Don't start with that," she pouted. "Think of it as an *investment*. I have an appointment with Mr Measles this evening and he says he's got a special surprise for me. I *have* to iron out these wrinkles!"

As if on cue, the machine hissed and puffed some more.

Caleb rolled his eyes. "But Measles..."

"I can handle Measles – he's putty in my hand. Don't worry, Caleb. I won't be giving you up to his silly little

C.A.S.H. scheme just yet. After all, you bring in the money driving Dad's old cab." She paused. "Mind you, the Cartwrights did buy a lovely piece of Spain with the pay-out they got for Myra…"

Caleb glared at her. Myra was his best friend. He hadn't seen her for months, ever since she had been exchanged to pay off her parents' debts. He missed her terribly.

"Don't make that face, Caleb. Things are just as wretched for me, you know. If your father hadn't vanished things would be different – if you want to blame someone, then blame *him*!" With that she swept out of the room.

Caleb was used to his mother flouncing around like a spoiled child. Leaving the plates on the table, he went up to his bedroom. After shutting the door, he stuck the Post-it note onto a collage of several months' worth of newspaper clippings reporting the disappearance of Bert Dallaway and the ensuing police investigation.

"The Red Lion," he muttered, "near the station, 4.30 p.m., Saturday 7th July."

He stood back and looked at a map of Fetherham hung next to the clippings. Could there be any link with this and

FETHERHAM

LOCAL FORCAST : FIAR MILD TON[...]ST NIGHT AND MORN[...]

LOCAL HISTORIA[...]
VANISHES

DALLAW[...]
CASE N[...]
CLOSE[...]

Today police strongly deni[...]
that the Bert Dallaway disa[...]
pearance case was closed d[...]
to lack of [...]. Earli[...]
repor[...] [...] resource[...]
we[...] [...]ched were reject[...]
by investigating officers w[...]
asserted that no unsolv[...]
case would be closed.

BANDONED CAB
VES NO CLUES AS TO
ER'S DISAPPEARANCE

t, Mr. Preside[...]

The Red Lion pub
near station
4.30pm
Saturday 7th July

TER

RE IS
TRAND
LAWAY?
VES ARE STUMPED

The search
for missing 43-year-
old Bert Dallaway is being
treated as a possible abduction.
While police are not ruling
anything out, after an extended
large-scale search of the area
and buildings surrounding
Fetherham station, they are
still confident Dallaway has
not been murdered. It is also
understood he was not prone to
drinking or d[...]

any other previous sightings of his dad? He had vanished so unexpectedly. Deep down, Caleb had the feeling he *must* be out there somewhere. He stared at the photo of his dad and Myra pasted to his mirror, and vowed never to give up looking.

His thoughts were interrupted by the doorbell ringing again. He slid out of his room. In the hallway below he could see Mr Measles, the family "banker", with his lizard-like features, pasty skin and cold beady eyes.

Measles presented Mopsy with a bouquet of flowers, which she seized with girlish glee, wafting him an airy kiss before taking his coat and leading him down the hall. Passing in front of the mirror, Measles stopped to smooth a bony hand over his carefully greased hair, causing it to slip over his left ear. He hurriedly put it back in place before following Mopsy into the lounge. Caleb stifled a snigger – Measles wore a wig!

Carefully he crept down the stairs and sat on the bottom step to listen.

"Well, I'm pleased to announce your latest loan has been approved," said Measles in a monotone drawl. He sounded anything *but* pleased – in fact he sounded as if he was about to die.

"Oh, thank you," Mopsy sighed. "I'm so relieved – we've had to cut back on so much. Bert really did leave us in a terrible mess."

"He was not the world's finest financial planner," Measles agreed. "Any news?"

"Not really. There's been another *possible* sighting, but it won't come to anything. It never does."

"Well, it's perfectly clear he's not coming back," blurted Measles. "Is your son still driving that cab?"

"Yes," replied Mopsy. "At least Bert did one thing right by teaching him how to drive."

"But unless Caleb works all God's hours, what he earns is not going to cover this fourth mortgage, Mrs Dallaway. And I need not remind you that a child driving a cab is highly illegal..."

"I realize that," said Mopsy in a strained voice, "but what can I do?"

"Well, your trump card, of course, is the C.A.S.H. scheme," said Measles eagerly. "Caleb would be very well looked after... Money Mongers positively *spoil* the children in their care."

"But how does it work *exactly?*" asked Mopsy, wringing her hands anxiously.

Measles shuffled in his seat. "C.A.S.H. stands for Children Acquired to Settle Home Loans. In return for writing off their clients' debts, the Money Mongers take possession of their children. They are housed in our permanent foundation where they are fed and clothed and educated in the way of modern-day financial services. It's a solid job for life – a win-win situation!"

"And what will become of Caleb if I decide to ... to go down this route?" Mopsy stammered, her voice low and timid.

"New recruits start their careers in cash machines, which introduces them to dealing with the public. At the same time they are assessed so they can be placed within the banking structure according to their strengths."

Mopsy nodded doubtfully. Measles patted her knee with his clammy white hand. "I assure you he will *thrive*. Caleb's a bright boy and could go far. Much further than he would on the outside, driving that cab for mere pennies. And you, Mrs Dallaway – *Mopsy*, if I may – can finally be free of all this financial worry, safe in the knowledge you've done the very best by your son…" Measles let his voice drift for dramatic effect, taking Mopsy to a place where money wasn't an issue and life was debt-free.

There were a few moments of silence before Caleb heard Measles flick open the catches on his briefcase and shuffle some papers. "Guess what these are," he said brightly.

"I can't think," Mopsy replied.

"What's the hottest show in town right now? Can't guess? Well," Measles announced slowly, for effect, "I have in my possession two tickets for *Prime Minister's Question Time – The Musical*. Aren't you excited?"

"Very," said Mopsy hesitantly.

"It's your *surprise* – my treat!"

"Should I change?"

"You're just perfect as you are, my dear..."

Caleb had heard enough. What planet was Measles from? He grimaced as he went back upstairs. On the way he noticed the empty face-press box and gave it an angry kick. There was only one thing for it: to keep out of the C.A.S.H. scheme and stand a chance of being reunited with his dad he'd have to work and work *hard*.

Shutting himself in his bedroom, Caleb began to put on his uniform – a long brown raincoat, a pair of beige brogues and a flat cap: his cab driver's outfit. He picked up a small red box, which he slipped into his pocket, then

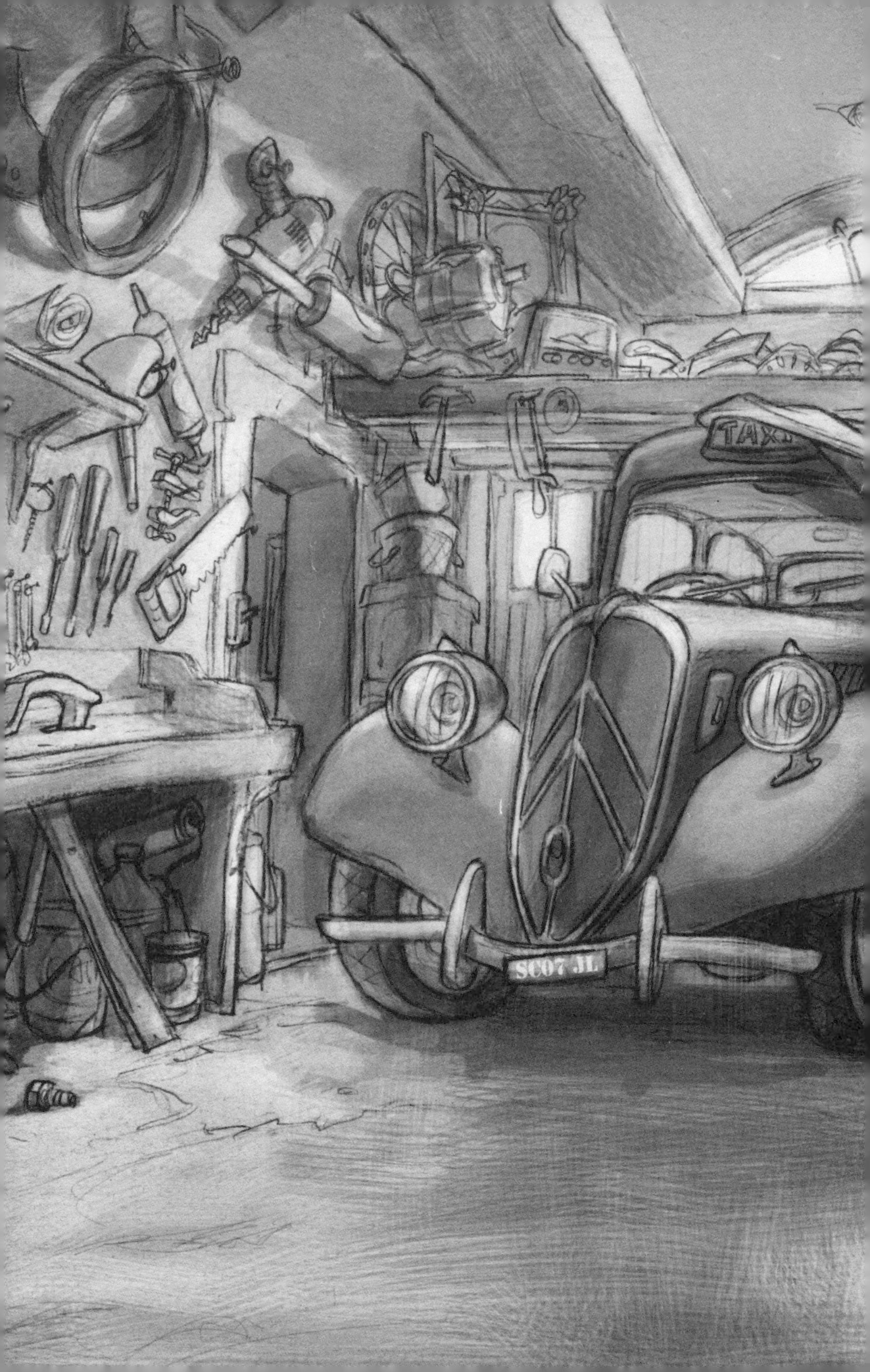
TAXI
SC07 JL

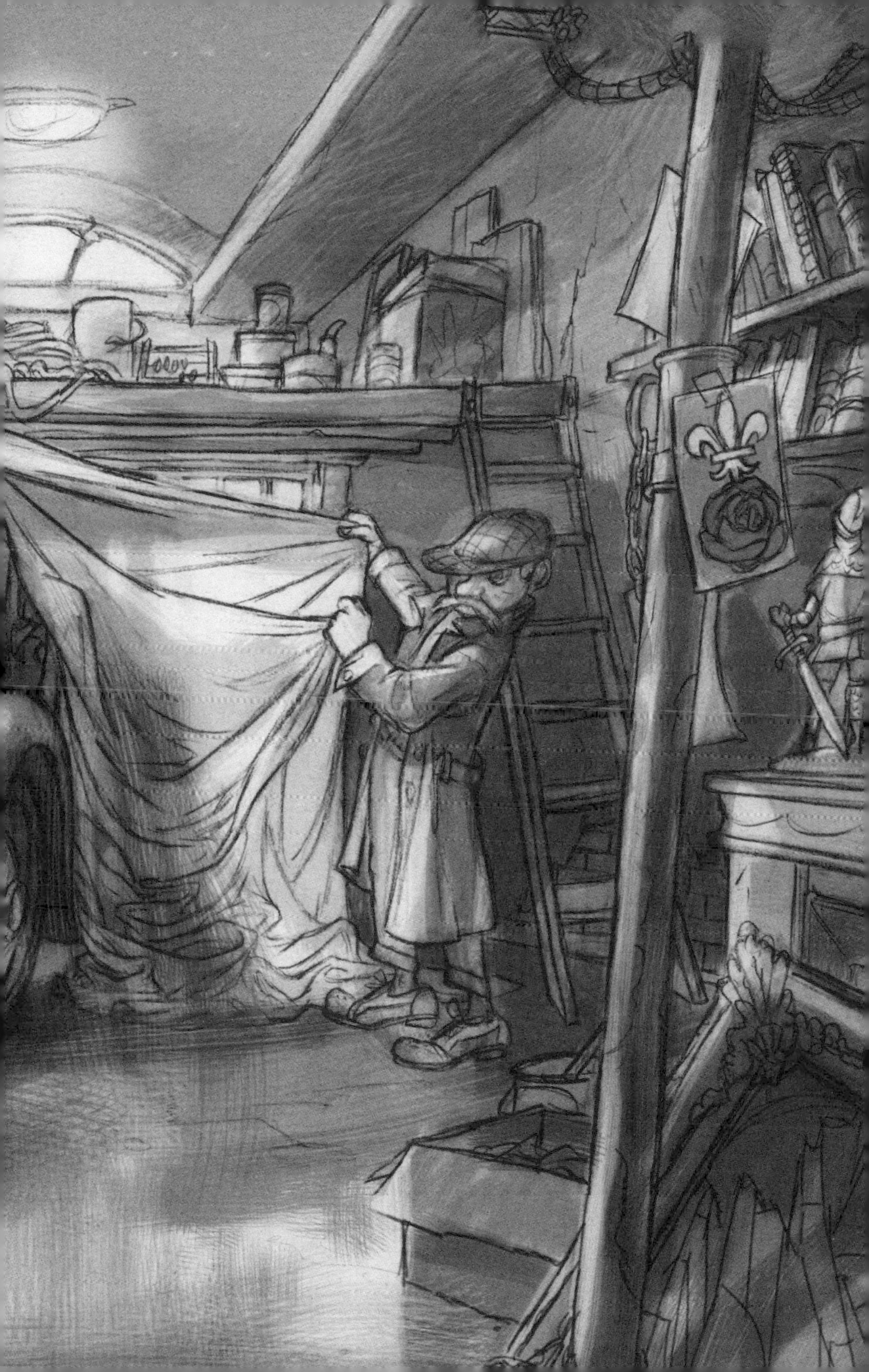

climbed out of the window and down the fire-escape steps to the garage below.

At one end of the garage was an area Caleb's father devoted to his study of medieval history, his passion. There was a sofa and a fridge and some metal-working equipment, and next to these, a large table supporting hundreds of tin soldiers. Bert had smelted the figures himself, carefully positioning the French and English armies to re-enact battles from the One Hundred Years' War.

At the opposite end of the garage was the famous cab.

Caleb flicked on a light and tore away the large dust cover. The cab was unlike any other car he had ever seen. It was his father's pride and joy. The vehicle itself was a vintage model, but the blue bodywork shone like a new penny. The seats were made of soft leather and the dashboard polished walnut. Inside it smelled of beeswax – and the wine-gums his father always kept in the glove compartment.

Having opened the garage door, Caleb climbed into the front seat. Making money from driving the cab was now his only means of avoiding being handed over to the Money Mongers – but he could not afford to get caught. As Measles had said, a minor in charge of a cab could get into all manner of trouble with the law. He took out the small red box from his pocket and selected a bushy false moustache, which he stuck carefully onto his lip with spirit-gum glue. Then, starting up the engine, he put the cab into gear and set off.

As he turned and drove carefully down the tree-lined avenue towards The Red Lion, Caleb checked his disguise in the rear-view mirror to make sure all was in place. Right now, he felt as if his whole life hung in the balance.

Chapter Two

Caleb made his way down the unkempt road. He grumbled at the litter-strewn pavements and gardens, and the rubbish that had drifted into piles at each side of the kerb. The whole of Fetherham had become a dump and it seemed there was no one left who cared. He fumed over the conversation between Mopsy and Measles. His dad would be horrified to know that the chief Money Monger had wormed his way into the house – and that he was taking his mum to a show! Caleb shuddered, his mind ringing with his dad's words: "Those wretched Money Mongers have only one ambition – to sustain their frenzied cycle of borrowing and lending, making the rich richer and the poor poorer. No son of mine will fall victim to those sick values!" But Caleb knew it was only a matter of time – especially now Mopsy had borrowed more money to splash out on a stupid face-press.

The only children who weren't in danger of being sucked

into the system were boys and girls from wealthy families. They roamed the streets in groups, making everyone's life a misery.

Driving past the park at the end of his street, Caleb's heart sank. The seats had been stolen from the swings, leaving sinister pairs of dangling chains. The roundabout had been vandalized beyond recognition and the little wooden hut at the top of the slide was covered in fresh graffiti:

Nervi belli pecunia infinita

(*Unlimited money is the muscle of war*)

Oh no, Caleb thought. *The slogan of the dreaded SODs.*

SODs, short for Spoilt Over-educated Delinquents, was how people referred to these mobs of bored rich kids who terrorized less-well-off areas for laughs. One particular gang, led by the infamous bully and mega-toff Piers Wooten-Maxwell, considered Caleb's neighbourhood its territory. Caleb knew they couldn't be far away when he spotted yet more graffiti:

Tu quam pepedisti oleis!

(*You smell like you farted!*)

Unfortunately he was right. At the far end of the park he spotted a bunch of SODs hurling cricket bats at the glass-roofed bandstand. A blubbery black Labrador lolloped about next to them, barking excitedly as a bat crashed to the ground, narrowly missing one of the boys.

"Mungo, you blithering idiot! You damn near had my head off!"

The SODs found this incredibly funny and started braying like donkeys.

"Call that bloody dog away! He'th walking all over the broken glath!" cried a boy with heavy eyelids and a pronounced lisp.

"Tarquin, come here, boy!"

"That's Piers's favourite dog! He better not have cut his paws, or you'll be for it!"

"He'll be all right. He's got his Burberry dog boots on ... nothing gets through those!"

At that moment a boy with sticking-out ears let off a firework and Tarquin took fright, tearing away across the park at full pelt.

"Marcus, you screw-pot! Catch that dog or Piers will kill you!"

They charged after the dog calling, "Tarquin! *Tarquiiin!!*"

Tarquin was fat and not that fast, so Caleb was surprised when he blundered out into the road in front of the cab. He slammed on the brakes just in time, missing the animal by a hair's breadth. The cab choked and then stalled, causing the terrified creature to let out an ear-piercing yelp before fainting as if dead.

"Oh, great," Caleb groaned. "This is all I need." Hurriedly he unbuckled his seatbelt and got out to take a look.

Marcus Eaton-Crestburly was the first SOD on the scene. He crouched in the road next to the dog, cradling its limp head in his arms. "You've *killed* him," he wailed, his mouth all wet and wobbly. He laid his wax jacket gently over the dog's body and snivelled uncontrollably.

"I didn't even hit him!" protested Caleb, putting on his deepest voice so as to maintain his disguise. "I'm sure he's just in shock. Let's get him out of the road."

"Don't you touch this dog, you working-class pleb!" Marcus screamed through his tears. "You're not fit to come anywhere

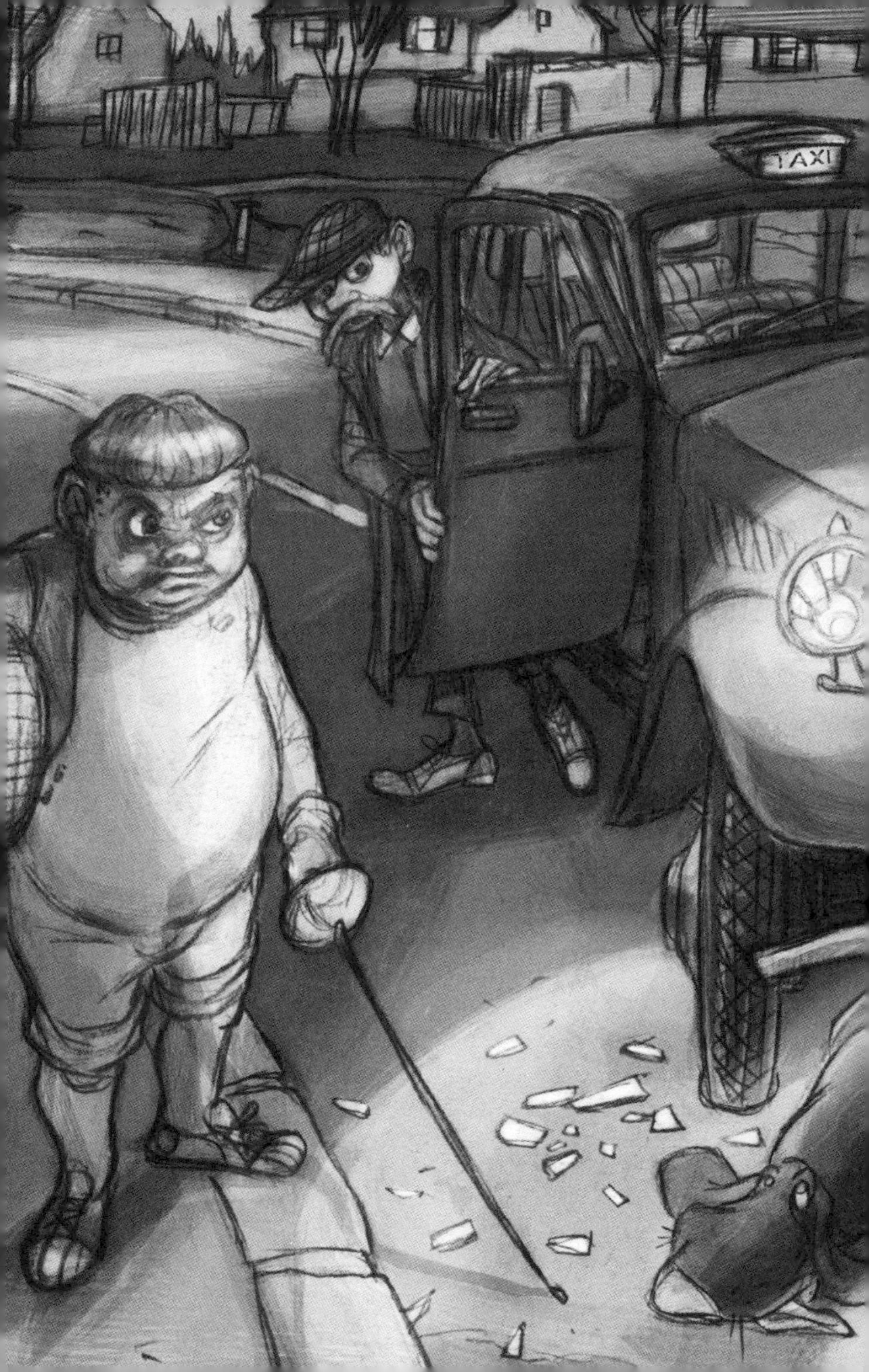
TAXI

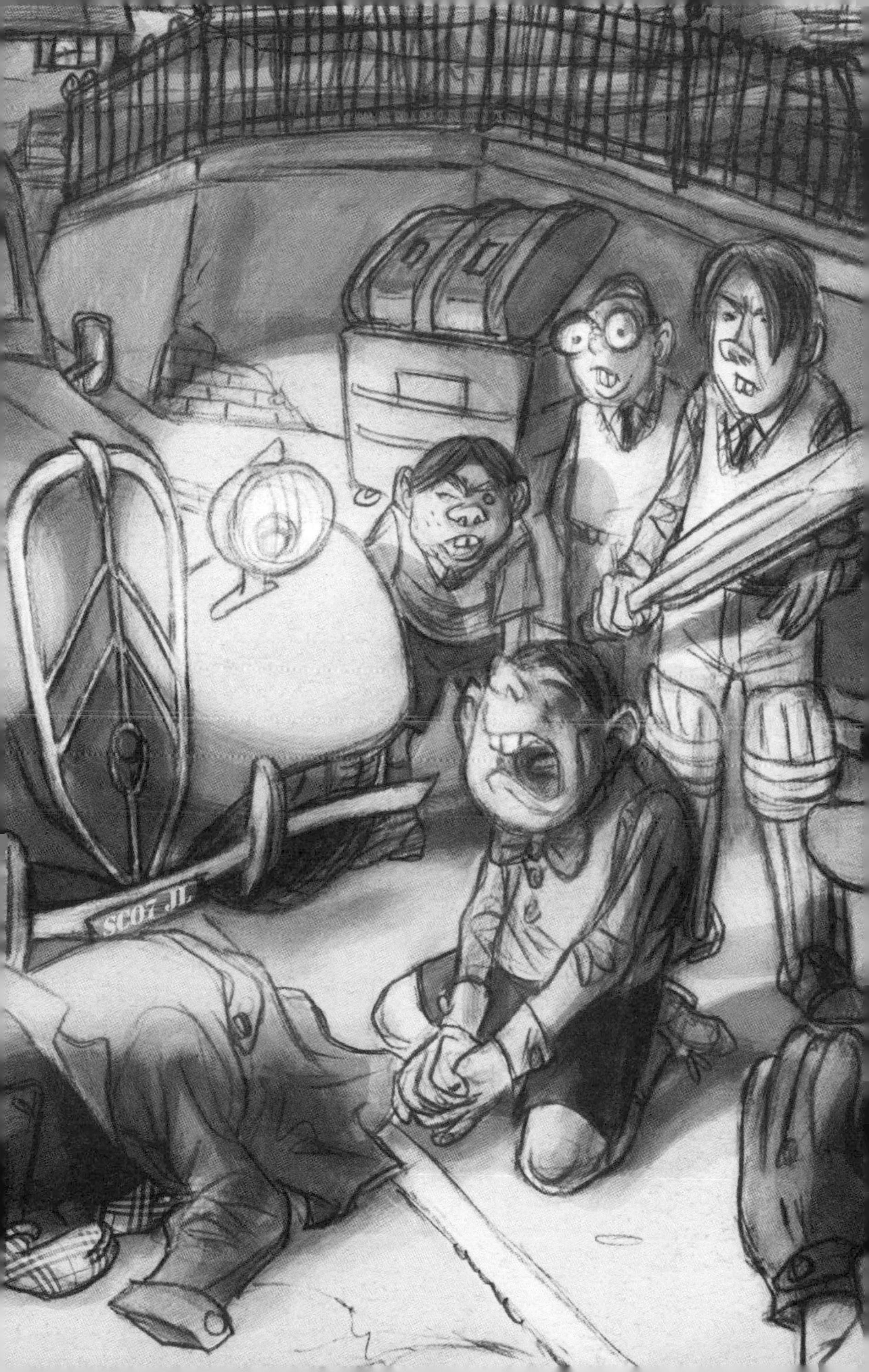
SC07 JL

near the likes of us! You disgust me with your meaningless existence and your dreary taxi and your" – he paused, searching for the right insult – "your flat, ugly, stupid cap!"

Caleb recoiled. By now the other boys had caught up and were heading straight for him. One particularly menacing-looking boy was slapping a cricket bat against his hand, slowly and with intent. Panicking, Caleb took a few discreet steps back towards his car.

"We all know your cab," a buck-toothed boy sneered. "You should be careful where you park it – you wouldn't want it to get broken now, would you? How could you *work* without it?" He spat out the word "work" as if it was the filthiest expression he knew. As if to punctuate the point, the boy with the bat swung it hard at one of the cab's headlights. It shattered, showering shards of glass onto Tarquin and the snotty-faced Marcus.

With perfect timing, Piers Wooten-Maxwell himself arrived, fresh, it seemed, from a fencing lesson. He still had his fencing foil strapped around his stocky body, and his auburn hair and freckled face were sticky with sweat. When he noticed Tarquin lying motionless in the road, covered in glass, he roared with rage. Caleb gulped and felt his knees go wobbly. The rest of the gang shrank back in fear.

"Why, you despicable *dog slayer*!" Piers drew his fencing foil with a flourish and lunged, musketeer-like, at Caleb, who fled to the door of the cab. He fumbled frantically with the handle, feeling the tip of the sword jab him in the back. Scrambling into the driver's seat, he clapped the door shut. Wooten-Maxwell took another lunge but this time the sword's point scraped against the cab's window, making a rasping sound like fingernails down a blackboard.

Caleb tried to stay calm as he turned the key in the ignition. "Come on! Come on!" But the cab was not one to be rushed. It grunted and shrugged before stalling again. Caleb gasped as Wooten-Maxwell's hand began rattling the door handle and his livid face squished up against the glass. Caleb pressed down on the lock and twisted the key once more. At last the cab shuddered into action and he let out a rush of breath. "You beauty!"

The cab lurched forward. Marcus leapt up suddenly from the road, tripping over Tarquin, who swiftly came round from his malaise. The dog sprung out from underneath the wax coat as if the incident had never happened and jumped excitedly to greet Piers. This resurrection was sufficient to distract the gang and allow Caleb to make his escape.

As he pulled away, he glanced in his rear-view mirror and saw the boys rejoicing in the street. Piers had taken hold of Tarquin's front paws. The dog was smothering its master's face with slobbery licks and they seemed to be dancing some kind of jig while Marcus, grinning widely, brushed the tyre marks off his coat.

Caleb sighed and switched on his windscreen wipers against the rain that was now falling. He noticed his hands were trembling. Piers's violent tantrums were infamous. It had been a close call.

Chapter Three

Caleb had lost valuable time getting to The Red Lion. He grumbled to himself as he drove on through the driving rain, almost overshooting a couple who were waving him down. He hesitated before deciding to pull over. If he could earn a few quid on the way to The Red Lion, all the better.

It wasn't until he got closer that Caleb noticed the couple were elderly. "Perfect!" he hissed under his breath, suddenly wishing he hadn't stopped. Old people were widely considered to be useless nut-cases, although Caleb was inclined to have a bit more time for them than most. After all, many of them had dreadful problems with achy legs and dizzy heads and for those reasons were dependable cab customers. But they were doddery and tended to dither about a lot and Caleb just wasn't in the mood today. What's more, they were notorious for their eccentric behaviour around children – especially in these days of C.A.S.H., when it was becoming uncommon to see kids about. The elderly could become quite excitable – violently so – when they caught a rare glimpse of a child. Caleb's disguise was deceptive, but he knew how vulnerable he would be if ever his cover was blown. Silently, he wound down his window, taking the decision to refuse the fare if they were going out of his way.

The couple, a man and a woman, were elegantly dressed – old, but not too decrepit. The man, in particular, had a jovial, round face and generous earlobes, which were half the size

again of his actual ears. They waggled mesmerizingly as he spoke. "The old bingo hall, please? Happy you came by. This rain is starting to come down hard…"

The bingo hall was a ten-minute drive across town to the south suburb near the station, not far from The Red Lion. Caleb nodded and the old man opened the door. He had just started the engine when suddenly there was a commotion behind him.

"I am not getting in *zis* cab!" cried the elderly woman. She sounded quite agitated.

"My dear, why on earth not?" the old man asked.

"Zis cab iz not safe – I know zis car and it iz dangerous."

The old man leaned towards Caleb's window. "Do you know this lady?" he asked.

Caleb strained his neck to get a better look at her. She was tall and slender with neatly bobbed grey hair poking out from a twenties-style cloche hat. She might have been attractive many years ago if it wasn't for a slightly "goosy" look to her.

"No," said Caleb, shaking his head. "I've never seen her before."

"Odd," said the old man. "She seems to know you – or at least your cab…"

The old man took his companion gently by the elbow and tried once again to guide her into the back seat, but she snatched her arm away. As she did so, her handbag flew to the ground and the old man scrambled to pick up her scattered possessions. Caleb was beginning to regret stopping. He tutted under his breath and glanced at his watch.

"Please, dear, do get in," the old man pleaded, handing her back the bag.

She seized it and promptly swiped him with it. "Sir!" she said. "I must inzist zat zis cab iz dangerous and I cannot get in!"

Caleb intervened. "I can assure you, madam, that this cab is perfectly safe. We'll be at the bingo hall in no time at all. You're getting quite wet fussing around on the kerb."

The lady peered through the window at Caleb. The scrutiny made him feel very uncomfortable. He instinctively stroked his moustache to make sure it was still in place.

"Well, maybe zis once," she said cautiously. "It wazn't you, in any case," she added. "Ze man driving zis car before waz younger zan you."

She reluctantly allowed her companion to settle her into the back seat. Once the door was shut, Caleb pulled away.

"Don't make any zudden movementz!" she warned.

"Of course not, madam," said Caleb.

"I do apologize," said the elderly man, leaning towards him and speaking in a quiet tone. "This lady is a recent acquaintance of mine. I've rather taken her under my wing. As you see, she is somewhat confused. I've been trying to find out where she comes from. Are you sure you haven't seen her before? It'd be damn useful if you had."

"Quite sure!" said Caleb firmly. "I think I would have remembered!"

They drove on in silence. Each time Caleb turned a corner the old lady clenched her fists and sucked air sharply through her teeth, grabbing at her friend's arm in terror. When Caleb reached to make a minor adjustment to his mirror she squealed in alarm and covered her eyes.

"Interesting vehicle," the old man commented at last. "Very beautiful... What's her story?"

Caleb felt pleased. He loved nothing more than talking about the cab. It felt like talking about his father. "My da—" He stopped himself short. "My *colleague* found the bodywork in Hamish McPower's scrapyard a few years ago and restored her.

She's a unique model so it was quite a puzzle putting her back together. Many of her parts had to be imported from France. McPower has a cousin with a yard over there – a Monsieur Poulnoir—"

"*Poul-noir,*" repeated the lady suddenly, causing Caleb to glance at her in the rear-view mirror. It was as if a light had gone on in her wrinkly old brain – like she was hearing something familiar that she couldn't quite place. Either that or she was simply, as Caleb was more inclined to believe, quite insane.

"Well, she's a unique vehicle indeed," said the old man. "I was in the motor industry all my working life and have never seen a model like her."

At last they pulled up outside the old bingo hall where a flashing sign read Tea Dance Today. Caleb watched as several ancient-looking couples dressed in their best outfits made their way up the steps.

The old man dug into his pocket, counted out the fare and said goodbye. "Madame Zis", as Caleb had unconsciously named the old lady, scrambled out of the cab as fast as her elderly frame could manage.

Once outside, she straightened her hat and looked up at the bingo hall, shaking her head slightly. "*Zut* – zis iz not how I remember it, not at all," she muttered.

Her companion patted her arm and led her up the steps, before turning back to Caleb, and, with a grin and a wink, tapping his temple with his forefinger. "Barking mad!" he mouthed.

Relieved to be rid of them at last, Caleb gave a small nod back. That should have been the end of that. But what happened next would change everything.

Chapter Four

Unlocking the glove compartment, Caleb took out the money box and quickly arranged the notes and coins the old man had given him. One coin didn't appear to fit anywhere though. Looking more closely, he realized he had never seen anything like it before. He took off his cap and held it up to the light. The coin was shiny and yellow, like real money, and certainly weighed quite a bit. It looked like foreign currency of some sort. The letters around the edge read The United Kingdoms of Franzingland. One side of the coin bore the portrait of a monarch wearing a jewel-studded beret and the other was marked 100 penny-francs.

Caleb sighed crossly and glanced at his watch. It had been almost two hours since the visit from Officer Lumley and if the lead at the pub was real, it would be going cold by now. But Measles's words echoed in his head:

"Unless Caleb works all God's hours, what he earns is not going to cover this fourth mortgage, Mrs Dallaway ... your trump card, of course, is the C.A.S.H. scheme..."

"Money is money, dammit," Caleb muttered to himself. He wasn't going to earn what he needed if customers paid him with phony coins! He knew he had to find the gentlemen and demand the correct fare even if it meant getting to The Red Lion Pub too late. He needed the money. He turned off the engine, undid his seatbelt and got out of the cab. He made his way up the stairs with the strange coin in the pocket of his raincoat.

Caleb had never been inside the bingo hall before. The foyer, which had once been majestic, was now shabby, with moth-eaten velvet curtains and threadbare carpets. Scores of old people mingled about, greeting each other. There was a queue at the coat check. Caleb turned up his collar and squeezed past a line of oldies, holding his breath against the sweet-and-sour odour of Werthers Originals and camphor.

Once in the main hall, where the dance was being held, he relaxed a little. The dim lighting worked better for his disguise. A single glitter ball rotated slowly, casting spots of different coloured light on the dancefloor. A few couples were already shuffling around to the music, provided courtesy of a small, bored-looking band in the corner of the room.

In another corner Caleb noticed a large trestle table covered with a mountain of mouth-watering delicacies. Plates dressed with frilly doilies were piled high with buns, sweets, petits fours, scones, pastries, biscuits, muffins, iced cakes, cream slices and fruit loaves. At the end of the table stood a large aluminium tea urn, and here he spotted Madame Zis and her friend pouring tea.

He walked over. The man squinted and fumbled for his glasses when he saw Caleb's small frame approaching. "I'm your cab driver," explained Caleb. "I just dropped you off."

"Ah, yes, the fella with the classic car. Wouldn't have thought this was your scene!" he chuckled, waving a liver-spotted hand towards the shuffling couples.

"I'm not here to *dance*," said Caleb, blushing slightly. "You gave me the wrong change…" He held out the offending coin.

The man slid his glasses to the tip of his nose and peered at it. "Heavens, what's that?" he exclaimed, picking up the coin and turning it between his thumb and forefinger. "Looks like something out of a child's board game…"

At once several heads turned sharply in their direction. Deaf though they might be, these crones were always keen and alert when children were mentioned. The very word "child" usually prompted an outpouring of some kind or other. This occasion was no exception.

A short lady standing nearby snapped open the clasp on her handbag and brought out a delicate pink handkerchief. She shook her head sorrowfully, the loose skin on her chin waggling like a turkey's gobbler. "Oh," she sobbed, dabbing her watery eyes, "it's been so long since I saw Sarah and Matthew. My poor darlings, how I miss them!"

"There, there, Doris," said another woman, with a face like a bag of burst balloons. She patted her friend's shoulder with a papery-skinned hand. "We all miss our grandchildren…"

"Ix shameful, thax what it ix!" interrupted another lady. An ill-fitting denture caused her to spit and spray as she spoke. "To think that I'd live to see the day when money meanx more to folk than their own flesh and blood!"

"If you want to hear a young un's voice these days, you have to go to one of them holes in the wall," her friend added resentfully.

"Zat iz it!" piped up Madame Zis. She slapped the top of the tea table decisively. "I knew zer was zomezing elze bizarre about zis town zese dayz! Where are all ze children?"

The others stared at her agog.

"What did you just say, dear?" said one old lady. "You know, what with that funny accent, it's hard to tell…"

Madame Zis tutted and repeated herself in strident tones. "I zaid, where are all ze children?"

The old man stopped examining the coin and glared at his companion in disbelief. "Have you had a blow to the head?" he asked.

"I hit my head in a car accident!" she said, touching the side of her temple. "I don't remember much after zat..."

"Then you don't remember that our grandchildren have all been exchanged for C.A.S.H.?" interjected another.

"C.A.S.H.?" Madame Zis replied hotly. "I don't know what you are talking about! My grandchildren are wiz zer mozer!"

"With their mother? Impossible!" said another, bristling with indignation. "Unless they're like them dreaded SODs—"

"Sodz? What are ze sodz? You are all talking rubbish!" Madame Zis flapped her hand dismissively.

"Bah – she ain't one of us," said a plump, balding man with a red face and a greasy comb-over. "She's one of them foreigners – French or something, if you fancy."

"French? French? What are you talking about? Ze French do not exist!" Madame Zis retorted.

There was sniggering and nudging.

"Ze French and English have been united for over six hundred years," continued Madame Zis, flustered. "What iz so funny?"

As the others began to mutter in confusion, Caleb noticed the frightened look in Madame Zis's eyes. Her companion shook his head slowly as if looking at a lost cause.

"Enough of zis, I'm going home!" she hissed at him.

"But where *is* your home, dear?" he asked.

"Not here!" She pulled away from him and made towards the exit.

The crowd watched in silence as Madame Zis strode out of the ballroom. Caleb, anxious to be on his way too, looked at his watch and cleared his throat.

"Ah, yes," said the old man rapidly, tearing his gaze away from Madame Zis's retreating figure. He tossed the foreign coin back to Caleb. "Well, you can keep that for starters … and take this for your trouble too," he added, shoving the right change into his hand.

"And have a cake, why don't you?" said an elderly woman, thrusting a plate of fondant fancies at him.

Caleb picked up one of the gooey pink mounds and took a large bite. It was glorious. "Thanks very much," he said, swiftly to leave. "Bye, then."

The old man was staring at him quite strangely. "I say, old chap," he said, out of the side of his mouth. "You seem to be having a spot of bother with your 'tache." He tapped the top of his lip surreptitiously.

Caleb's hand flew up to his face. It was bare! Hairless!

The old man coughed slightly and nodded in the direction of the half-eaten fondant fancy. Draped over the sticky pink icing like a hairy caterpillar sat Caleb's moustache.

Horrified, Caleb clamped his hand over his top lip. But it was too late. Eagle-eyed Doris had spotted him. She whipped his hand away, exposing his youthful – and now much reddened – face.

"*Run for it, boy!*" whispered the old man urgently.

"A CHILD!" wailed Doris, causing the band to stop and the lights to inexplicably go up. "A *real child!*"

Pandemonium ensued as dozens of grandchild-deprived old people lunged for Caleb.

"Ooooh, he's perfect...!"

"Let me touch him..."

"Come here to grandma, sonny..."

"Mable, come and see! It's a boy – an actual BOY!"

Someone whipped off Caleb's flat cap and, before he knew it, countless hands were ruffling his hair. More arms reached out, trying to hug him and, worse still, several pairs of old lips puckered up to plant sour-breathed kisses on his hot cheeks. Caleb snatched back his cap and wriggled and writhed, trying to escape a surprisingly strong grip. One woman shrieked and fainted. Another, predicting casualties, called for the paramedics.

Caleb lunged forward, unbalancing a sufficient number of elderly people to make a small gap in the crowd. He ran, tearing down the foyer steps three at a time, before stumbling at the bottom. As he struggled to regain his balance, the shrill babble of his pursuers rang in his ears. He pushed at the door and staggered out into the welcome cold of the evening. Madame Zis was lingering on the steps, holding her coat tightly around her. She glared at the moustache-less Caleb as if another confusing thing was more than she could bear.

Caleb gave a loud hoot of triumph as he reached the cab and grabbed at the door handle. He yanked it open and fumbled for his keys. At last he dug them into the car's ignition and slammed the door.

A few of the more agile oldies were gaining on him. Caleb glanced up and saw Madame Zis being jostled by the advancing mob. She was holding onto her hat, trying not to be swept down the stairs by the unsteady tide of geriatrics. Caleb's heart thudded in his chest as he changed up a gear and hurtled away. In his rear-view mirror he could see the throng spilling out onto the street.

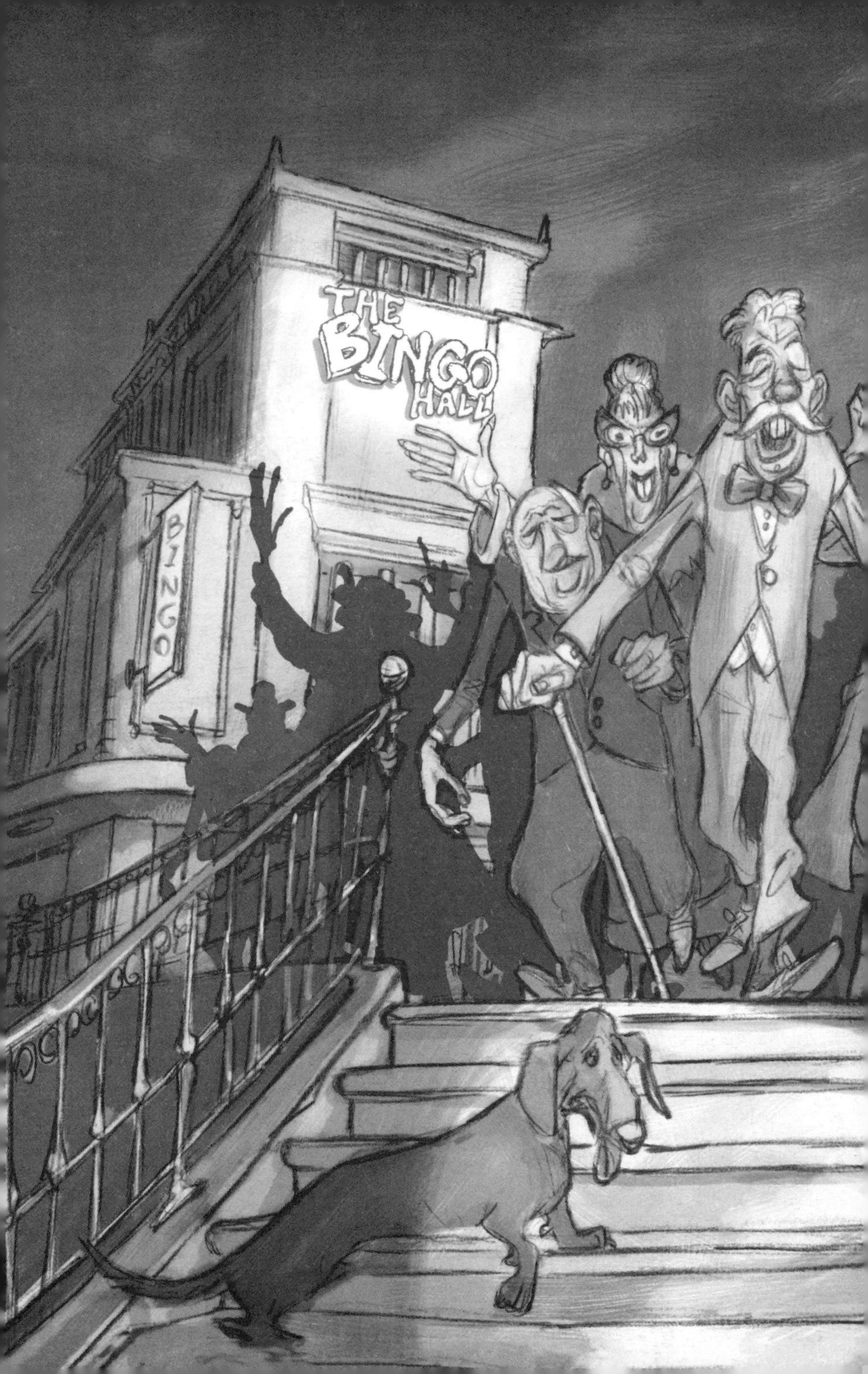
THE BINGO HALL
BINGO

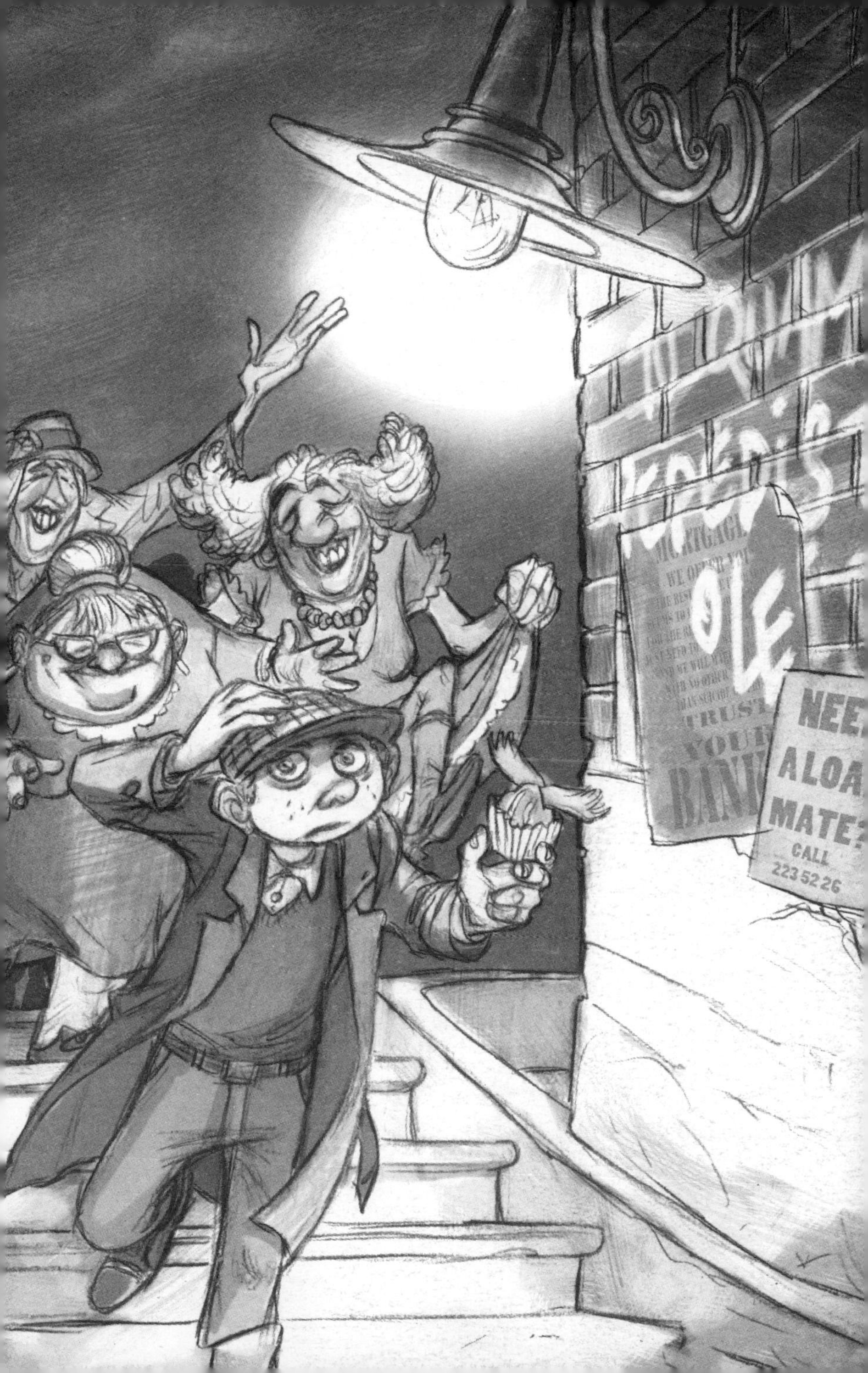
NEE
ALOA
MATE?
CALL
223 52 26

But suddenly, his pounding heart seized tight and almost stopped when he noticed the road in front of him was entirely blocked by gas works. His hands shaking, he executed a masterful three-point turn. Then he forced his foot down on the pedal, accelerating back towards the bingo hall as fast as the cab could go.

The elderly mob showed no sign of budging as Caleb drew closer. Several of them stood obstinately in the middle of the road, waving their hands in the air. This game of chicken lasted a few torturous seconds before Caleb gave in. With seconds to spare he heaved a hard left on the steering wheel, narrowly avoiding mowing them down.

What happened next took mere moments but seemed to last an eternity. As the cab swerved violently, Caleb glided across the smooth leather of the front seat. At the same time the steering wheel, which appeared to have come clean off in his hands, slid across with him. He heard cries of dismay and, in ghastly slow motion, saw the blurred faces of the old people outside. Then he felt the cab pitch and reel as if it had hit something.

Chapter Five

Caleb wasn't sure how many minutes had passed. His hands were still wrapped tightly around the steering wheel, while a strange whistling rang in his ears. He stared at his bone-white knuckles in silence before glancing down at his legs for signs of blood or breakage. Once he was confident he had not been injured, he had the terrible thought that someone else might have been. Perhaps he had hit someone?

Feeling sick, he opened the door. There was a horrible grating sound. The right-side wing of the car had been damaged, but to his surprise and relief none of the elderly mob was anywhere to be seen. As he stood, dazed, in the middle of the road, another car passed, giving him a wide berth and tooting gently to warn him to get out of the way. Caleb stepped onto the pavement and looked up, blinking curiously at the neon sign on the building. It looked just like the bingo hall, but something was different… The spelling was all wrong:

Caleb got back in his cab and examined himself in the rear-view mirror. In times of uncertainty he always liked to have a good look at his face. It was reassuring and familiar. His flat cap had been hurled from his head during the crash and his curly hair was sweaty and dishevelled. His top lip was still moustache-less but thankfully his pale face was without a blemish and there were no signs of bumps, gashes or bruises.

He smoothed his hair with the palm of his hand, put his flat cap back on and replaced his moustache with one of the spares he kept in the small red box. The interior of the car was intact, aside from the fact that the steering column had mysteriously switched sides. Caleb hauled and pushed at it, trying to move it back into position, but it was stuck tight.

He breathed in deeply and stuffed a handful of wine gums into his mouth, hoping the sugar would help calm his jangling nerves. Then he turned the ignition and coaxed the cab into life.

As the engine coughed and spluttered, Caleb discovered a shoebox full of his father's tin soldiers had become dislodged from under the seat and was blocking the gear stick. He picked it up, replaced the lid properly and put it next to him before pulling away towards the high street.

He had only gone a short way up the road when a driver raced towards him on the same side of the road. Caleb had to swerve to avoid hitting him. The driver honked his horn and gestured wildly. Caleb honked and gestured back.

Something was up.

The cab made an unnerving, grinding noise as Caleb braked at the traffic lights, and as he sat there staring into the early-evening gloom, he was struck by two extraordinary phenomena. Firstly, everyone was driving on the wrong side of the road. Secondly, there was now a *tramway* on Fetherham High Street. He stared in disbelief as a smart red tram glided by, its bell *ting-ting*ing brightly.

That wasn't there before, he puzzled.

Another car, arriving head-on, honked impatiently, blaring its headlights. Giddy with confusion, Caleb put the cab into gear and pulled away, manoeuvring to the opposite lane to follow the tail lights of the car in front. He drove cautiously, feeling suddenly unsure of his driving skills. Around him, the street lights were coming on one by one, revealing a high street that was entirely transformed.

There were no whitewashed display windows or boarded-up shop fronts; no 'To Let' signs or 'Going into Liquidation' notices, which Caleb was so accustomed to seeing. Instead there were colourful window displays of wooden crates filled with fruit and vegetables, stores selling baby clothes, bookshops, cafés, travel agents, delicatessens and butcher's shops with large, succulent hams hanging in the window. And everywhere looked so *clean*. Where were the polystyrene chip cartons, coke cans and carrier bags that normally littered the pavements? The pedestrian areas were planted with trees and all the rubbish was neatly binned.

But what struck Caleb most was the *people*. He saw families out together. There were couples with pushchairs, parents with their arms draped affectionately over their children's shoulders – and others holding hands with excitable toddlers. Adults and children sat together at tables sharing meals and drinks, *talking* to each other. Caleb couldn't remember *ever* seeing such a spectacle. He had no memory of walking down the high street with his mother. In fact he couldn't remember the last time his mother walked *anywhere*.

It all seemed so odd.

Caleb was forced to abandon his gawping as he realized the cab was struggling. The grinding noise was getting deeper and more insistent. He had to think along more practical lines. He headed in what he hoped was the direction of the scrapyard, situated near the old abandoned airfield and Fetherham sewage works on the opposite side of town. No one, other than his father, knew more about the cab than Hamish McPower, and Caleb desperately wanted to see a familiar face.

But when he reached the other side of town, Caleb was astounded to find a neat airstrip with rows of light aircraft and a handful of helicopters. Where the sewage works had once stood there was an impressive array of modern office buildings set in smart, landscaped grounds.

What on earth was going on?

Luckily Caleb found the scrapyard where he had hoped it would be. He stopped in front of the caravan that served as an office and a middle-aged man wearing a pair of old jeans and a grubby red jumper came out, wiping his fingers on an oily rag.

"Excuse me, is Mr McPower here?" asked Caleb, getting out of the cab.

"*Mais non* – he iz not *here*," the man replied, in a tone that suggested he found the question absurd.

"Not here?" Caleb repeated.

"*Mais non!* You know him?"

"He's a friend of the family," said Caleb.

The man jerked his head slightly and a pair of spectacles hopped from the top of his head down onto his nose. He peered through them at Caleb. He had an imposing pair of eyebrows and his breath smelled strongly of aniseed. Caleb stroked his moustache to reassure himself that it was still attached. For a moment the man looked puzzled, as if he was struggling to remember something. Caleb squirmed nervously and pointed to the damaged wing of his cab.

"Hmm, let'z zee..." The man crouched to examine the underside of the car, grunting and muttering to himself. "It seemz worze zan it iz," he said finally, standing up. He looked at his watch. "Iz zis urgent?"

"It is a bit," said Caleb, biting his bottom lip.

"I need an hour. Come back and I'll have it done."

With that the man turned his back on Caleb and went back into his office.

Odd that he didn't take my name, thought Caleb. *He didn't seem to think there was anything remarkable about the cab either. Most people do.*

There had been a familiarity in the mechanic's manner that Caleb could not quite place. Puzzling over the encounter, he took a shortcut he knew across the airfield towards the town centre. The tarmac runway was smooth and even – totally unlike the stretch where Caleb had learned to drive, which had been riddled with cracks and overgrown tufts of grass.

His thoughts were soon interrupted by a soft humming noise above him. He craned his neck to look. A titanic airship glided gracefully several thousand feet up, its port and starboard lights glinted against the violet sky. It was heading towards a horizon of tall, crystalline skyscrapers.

"Wow!" gasped Caleb. "Since when have there been airships and skyscrapers in Fetherham?" It all seemed so unfamilar. He had no idea what to make of it all.

He might have stood and gazed for longer at the extraordinary sight, but it was getting dark, and he only had an hour to find out where he was and, more importantly, how to get home and follow up the lead at The Red Lion.

He hurried back towards the town centre, becoming increasingly confused by his surroundings. The houses were taller than he was used to, with brightly coloured shutters at the windows. Children played in the gardens and delicious cooking smells wafted on the air. Arriving in the town square, he found it strangely pristine, with elegant trees decorated in bunting. The whole atmosphere was livelier and happier than Caleb had experienced before.

In the centre of the square was a stall selling newspapers

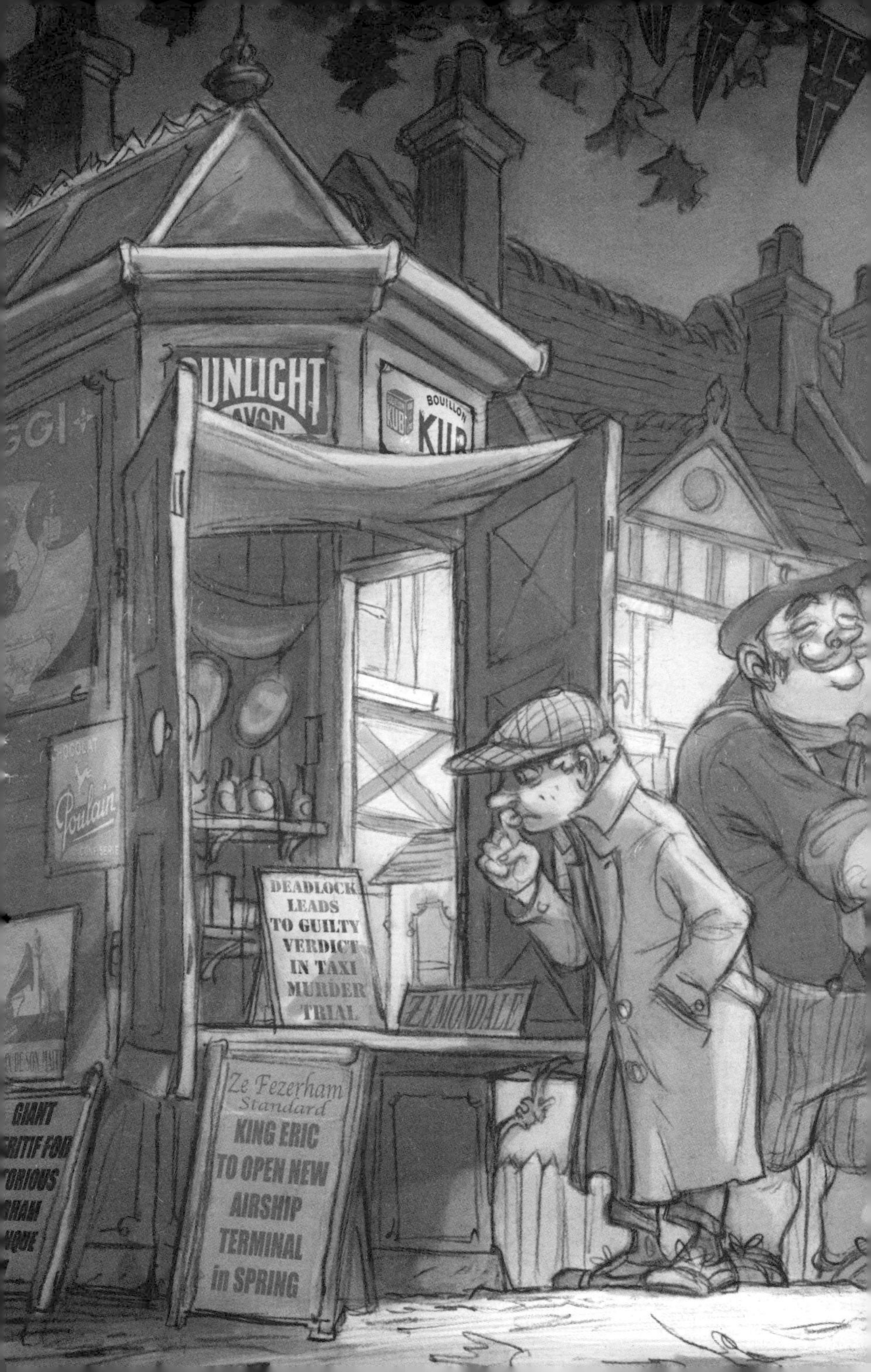
BOUILLON
KUB
Poulain
DEADLOCK LEADS TO GUILTY VERDICT IN TAXI MURDER TRIAL
Ze Fezerham Standard
KING ERIC TO OPEN NEW AIRSHIP TERMINAL in SPRING
GIANT

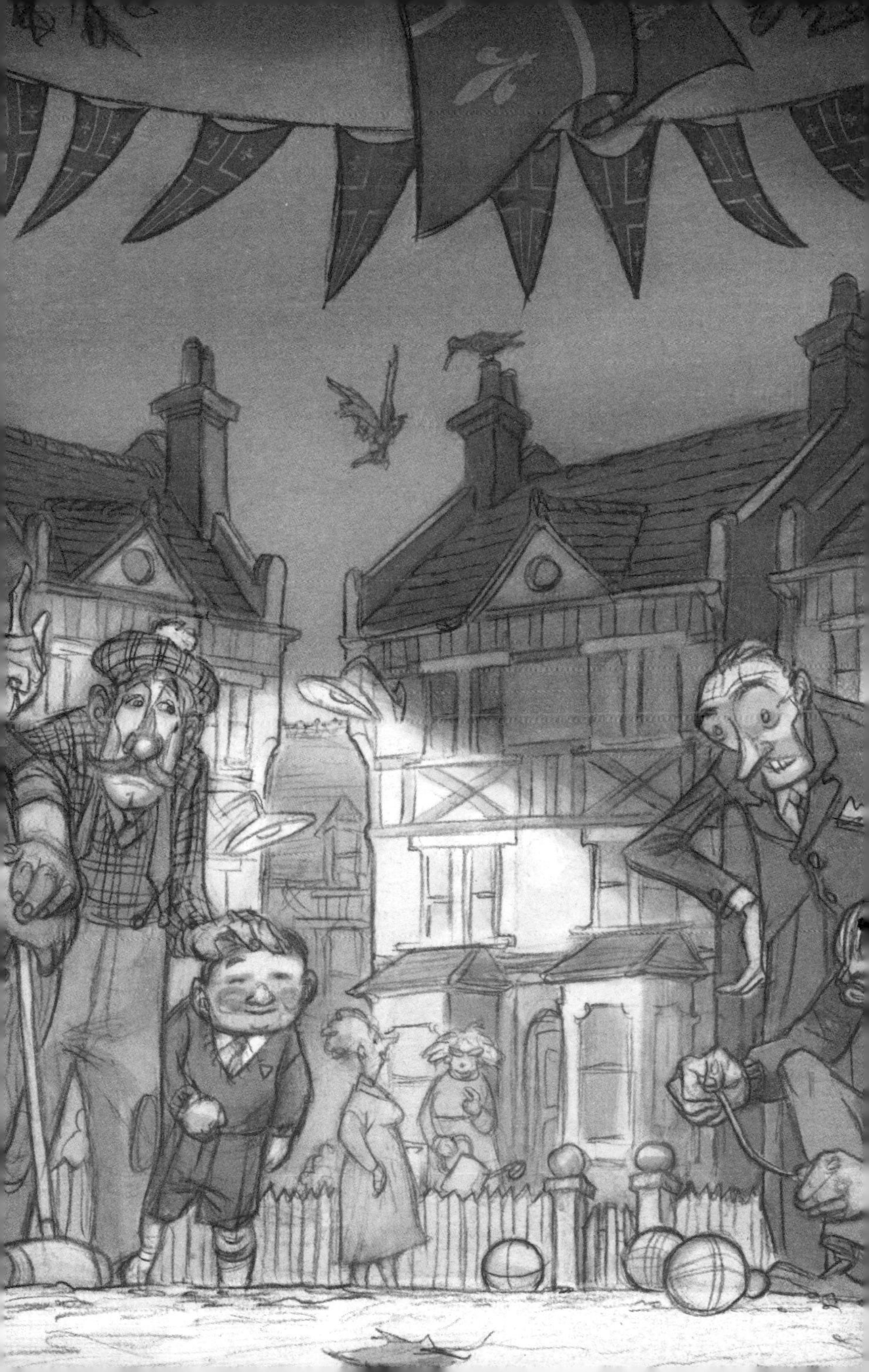

and magazines. The stall keeper was a round and jovial-looking man wearing a maroon beret and a cotton scarf knotted around his neck. He was dressed in baggy trousers held up with braces and a faded checked shirt – unlike the clothes worn by anyone Caleb knew. He stood a few metres from his stall, clacking together a pair of what looked like cricket balls. More men, similarly equipped, milled about nearby, joking and laughing heartily.

Caleb sidled up to the stall and darted behind a vertical newspaper stand so as not to draw attention to himself. At that moment, a tall man tossed a little wooden ball in the air, which landed some distance from the group of men. He traced a semi-circle in the gravel with the heel of his shoe, dropped a ball behind the line and picked up a heavy, long-handled mallet.

What is this game? Caleb wondered. *Where am I?* He scanned the titles in the newspaper display, hoping for some kind of clue. *Ze Daily Post, Z'Xpress, Liberation, Ze Mondale.*

Caleb didn't recognize any of them – but then something familiar caught his eye.

Ze Fezerham Standard.

He snatched up the newspaper and cast an eye over the headlines:

Just then a roar erupted from the group in the square. "Zavier! Sacred *palouf*!"

There was much muttering and shuffling as the teams stepped back to allow a young man to study the formation of the balls. Slowly he bent his knees and swung the mallet between his legs. The ball flew into the air. There was a breathless silence and both teams watched as it landed on an opponent's ball, sending it skittering across the gravel.

"CARREAU!!" the winning team cried.

The others groaned in despair.

There was some good-natured shoving before one of the men spotted Caleb, who was peering out from behind his copy of *Ze Fezerham Standard*.

"Heh, Claude, you have a customer..."

The stall keeper raised his eyebrow. "Can I help you wiz somezing, monsieur?"

Caleb lowered his eyes and shook his head quickly. He stuffed the newspaper back in its stand and scuttled away to the other side of the square. His heart beat faster. *What world was this – and why was everyone speaking like that old woman, Madame Zis?*

He slowed down as he came to an inviting-looking bistro that, in the Fetherham he knew, was a dingy fish-and-chip shop. The menu displayed outside caught his eye. *What in the name of all things culinary was this?* He could hardly believe the gastronomic mish-mash swimming before his eyes:

Evening Specialz

❧ ◦ ☙

Snail and mushroom pie wiz purée potatoez and onion gravy

Beef Bourguignon wiz Yorkshire pudding and horseradish sauce

Battered frogz legz wiz chipz, mushy peaz and a pickled egg

It had to be a joke? These concoctions made Caleb's kitchen creations appear positively gourmet!

Sitting at a table outside the bistro was a group of boys, a little older than Caleb. They were laughing and chatting while drinking hot chocolate. They all wore uniforms and identical scarves embroidered with a green-and-blue motif. He could just make out the words:

FEZERHAM GRAMMAR SCHOOL

Caleb had attended Fetherham Grammar, but once the Money Mongers's C.A.S.H. scheme was launched, the school had shut within six months.

"You going home?" he heard one boy say to his friend.

"*Non*, I'm going to the library to finish my geography project," was the woeful reply. "Mr Smiz will kill me if I'm late wiz it again." He stood up, slung his bag of books over his shoulder and prepared to leave.

Fetherham's library had closed around the same time as the school. It was now a boarded-up shell of a building with graffiti on the walls, a vast hole in the roof and pigeons nesting on the disused shelves. But if *this* library was open, then perhaps Caleb could learn more about where he was without attracting attention.

Caleb followed the boy across the square towards a grand, pillared building, with glass doors and wide stone steps leading to the entrance. The library was fully lit inside and he could see it was crammed with bookshelves and bustling with activity. Caleb was sure he could find out all the information he needed here. But just as he was about to climb the steps, his attention was caught by a flyer pinned to the noticeboard. A face was staring out at him and he recognized it immediately.

Madame Zis!

Chapter Six

MISSING PERSON

Have you seen **Odette Ocelot**? Last seen leaving ze library on ze evening of 12 November and getting into a taxi with zis man...

Below the photograph of Madame Zis was an artist's impression of a forty-something man with curly hair, round glasses and a cleft chin. Caleb swallowed hard. The drawing looked like his father, who had gone missing that very same day. He carefully unpinned the weatherworn notice and grasped it tightly. He could hardly contain his excitement at finding a clue to his father's whereabouts.

Halfway up the steps Caleb passed a young man who was busking. His instrument resembled a pennywhistle coupled with a set of bellows, which he pumped under his arm like an accordion. He was playing a rousing *rum-pa-pa, tiddly-tiddly-toot* type of tune, his head dipping and body pitching in time with the music. Caleb stopped to look again at the notice in his hand and, as he did so, collided with the busker's open instrument case, sending its contents of coins scattering.

"Hey, *imbecile!*" the busker barked. "Watch where you're going!" He put down his instrument and began to pick up the coins.

"I'm so sorry," babbled Caleb, "let me help you."

He scampered up and down the steps, picking up as many coins as he could. They were bright yellow and shiny, just like the one he had been given earlier. He tipped them back into the velvet-lined case, mumbled an apology and continued up the steps.

He felt full of hope as he pushed the library door and went in.

A skinny lady with a long neck and wire-framed glasses stood behind the reception desk. She smiled as Caleb approached, cocking her head to one side like a curious bird. Caleb held out the notice for her to see. His hands were shaking.

"Excuse me, do you know if this woman has been found?" he asked, trying to keep his voice calm.

The lady frowned as if she was having trouble understanding his accent. "Excuze me?"

Caleb pointed to the photo of Madame Zis. "Has she been found?" he repeated.

The librarian looked at the picture and became overwhelmed with emotion. Gulping tiny mouthfuls of air like a stranded fish, she reached for a box of tissues. She blew her pointy nose, making a small trumpeting sound and shook her head woefully.

"Do you know this woman?" Caleb asked again. "I think I might have met her recently. She's tall and wears a green felt hat. She's a little..." he hesitated, "...a little confused. Some might say eccentric – or *unhinged* perhaps?" He tapped his temple with his forefinger.

"*Monsieur!*" the woman hissed. "Madame Ocelot iz one of the greatest academic historians of our time. What are you talking about? *Unhinged?* Never!" Tears sprung from her eyes and she sniffed into her tissue before composing herself again. "Madame Ocelot researched here in zis library. Look," – she pulled out a book from under the reception desk – "zis waz published just before her dizappearance."

Caleb turned the thick volume over in his hands. The title read *The Reign of Queen Jeanne – From Maid to Monarch*. There was a black-and-white picture of Madame Zis on the inside sleeve. She did look clever in this photo – much cleverer than she did in real life.

He lowered the book and drew the lady's attention back to the artist's impression of his father. "Do you know who this is?" he asked.

The librarian looked at Caleb as if he had just dropped out of a tree. "Mais, zat iz Bertrand Dallaway, of courze – ze monster guilty of doing away wiz zis poor woman. You don't read ze newspapers?" She waved a copy of *Ze Fezerham Standard* at Caleb and pointed to the headline:

DEADLOCK LEADS TO MURDER CONVICTION IN TAXI DISAPPEARANCE TRIAL

"He waz arrested some days after she waz reported missing," she continued. "He iz found guilty today!"

Caleb's chest tightened as if an icy hand was squeezing his heart. "What will happen to him?" he asked, his voice so choked that he could scarcely speak louder than a whisper.

"Why, he getz what every assassin haz coming to him. He will be executed!"

"Executed?!"

"Yez – he dies by guillotine at ze town hall in three weeks' time. And good riddance to him!"

Caleb sat down on a nearby chair. He rubbed his hair and tried to calm his racing thoughts. Madame Zis's book trembled in his hands and, as he looked at it, he knew at once what he had to do. There was no time to lose if he was to see his father again.

Chapter Seven

"Can I borrow this?" Caleb asked the librarian, holding out the copy of Madame Zis's book.

"I'll need to see your library card, please," she replied.

"I don't have one," said Caleb.

The woman positioned herself in front of a computer. "Zat iz no problem. We can do you one right now. I need to take a few details... Your name?"

"Caleb Dallaway."

The woman looked up sharply and peered at Caleb through narrowed eyes. She took a deep breath before typing into her computer. "Address?"

Caleb faltered. "24 Pennant Road, *Fezerham,*" he said, trying his best to imitate the accent.

The woman pulled out a Polaroid camera and a few moments later Caleb was in possession of a brand-new, laminated library card bearing his picture. He took out the copy of Madame Zis's book and then, when the librarian was distracted, folded *Ze Fezerham Standard* under its front cover.

Glancing at the giant clock in the entrance hall reminded Caleb it was time to go and collect the cab. He hurried through the network of shortcuts and alleyways that led to the airfield. He arrived at the scrapyard hot and out of breath. He had been clinging so hard to the book that his hand ached.

The mechanic was making some last adjustments.

"Have you heard about the Dallaway case?" blurted Caleb as the man revved the engine.

"But, of course, it'z all over the newz," he replied.

"Do you think he did it?" asked Caleb.

The mechanic shrugged his shoulders. "He iz found guilty. What bizness iz it of mine?"

"They say he will be guillotined," Caleb continued.

The mechanic shrugged again and, pouting, made a fart noise with his lips. "Zat iz ze punishment for zis kind of crime," he replied, matter-of-factly.

Caleb's spirits sank. Was he the only one horrified by

the barbarous act of chopping off someone's head?

"Zere – she iz done." The mechanic dropped the bonnet of the cab. "Zat will be 3,258 penny-francs. Shall I write you an invoice?"

Caleb's mood swung from shock to despair. He had overlooked the fact he would have to pay for the repairs. He opened the car door and fumbled blindly around in the glove compartment for the money box, at the same time knocking over his father's box of tin soldiers. He grabbed the coin Madame Zis's companion had given him and held it out hopefully. "I'm sorry but I appear to have come out without my wallet," he said. "Is this enough?"

But the mechanic wasn't listening. His eyes were fixed like lasers on the spilled tin soldiers. "Zose are valuable goods to be leaving in your car like zat," he said.

"They were made by my father," said Caleb, momentarily forgetting his disguise.

"Well, he wouldn't be pleazed to know zey are all over ze ground like zat," said the mechanic, bending to pick them up. "Why! Zey are *mag-nif-ique*!" He turned one of the figures round in his oil-stained fingers. "Why do you keep zese priceless pozzessions in ze car like zis?"

Caleb didn't quite understand the question. "Because it's a cab," he answered. "I have to keep all my fares in the cash box." He tried once more to offer the coin, but the mechanic nudged his hand away. He pointed to one of the tin soldiers.

"I could maybe take one of zem az payment?"

Caleb was taken aback. "Just one? You can have more if you want…" He picked up a handful of soldiers and thrust them towards the man, who recoiled and shook his head.

"*Zut alors!* I am an honest mechanic, not a robber!" He looked suspiciously at Caleb. "Zey say a fool and hiz money are easily parted!" He took a small soldier carefully from Caleb's hand and pocketed it in his overalls. "You had better put all zose away and get zem home safely," he added, nodding at the rest of the figures. "It iz madness to carry such large amounts around like zat."

He grumbled a farewell, leaving Caleb to put the lid on the box of tin soldiers and place it back under the seat.

The cab purred contentedly as he drove away from the scrapyard. There was no sign of the ugly grating sound. Once he was out of the gates, Caleb turned towards the airfield, which he was hoping would now be empty of planes and people. Not quite so. Most of the lights in the hangars were out but there were still one or two people milling around.

A sole light aircraft buzzed overhead preparing to land. But there was no time to pay heed. Caleb figured that wherever he was, there was only one way of getting back – and that was the cab. He had to make the cab do what it had done before. He needed to recreate the same scene that had happened in front of the bingo hall.

Caleb pulled up at the top of the runway and revved the engine. He shoved his foot down hard on the accelerator pedal to reach top speed. His heart pounded as he reached the end of the runway and yanked on the steering wheel. The tyres screeched. Caleb felt the cab wobble onto two wheels before thumping back down on the tarmac.

Nothing happened.

He tried again and again, before finally careering onto the grass in a spectacular 360 degree spin.

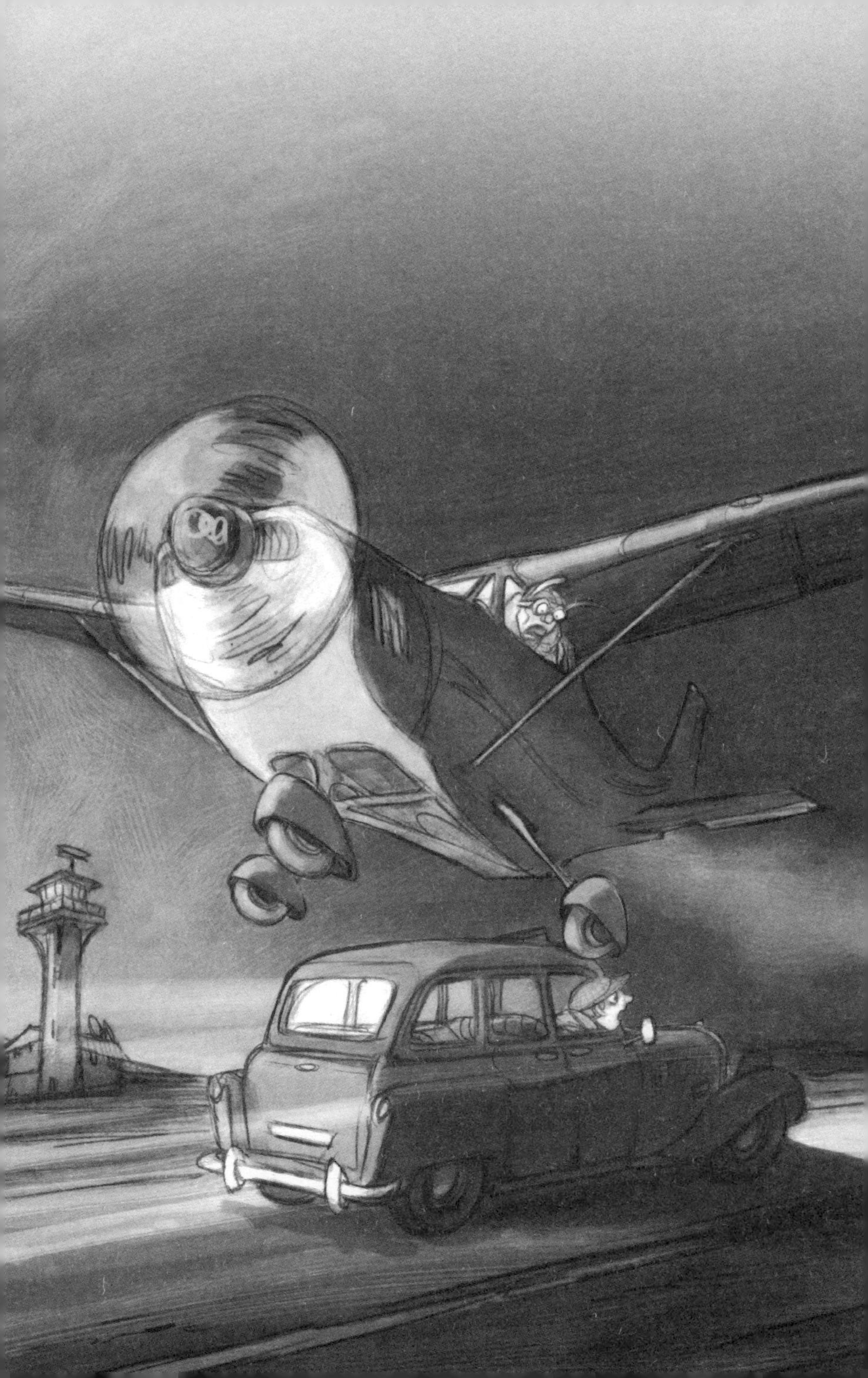

Caleb could smell burning rubber and the temperature gauge was nudging into the danger zone. He sat for a few moments to let the engine cool and think back to what exactly had occurred outside the bingo hall.

Maybe I'm going too fast? he thought.

He tried again, this time keeping to a steady speed. Perhaps the secret was in the swerve? Fixing his eyes ahead, he imagined the gang of old ladies waving their arms and focused on an imaginary point. Then *bam!* he jerked down hard on the steering wheel. There was a violent surge as the wheel leapt to the other side of the dashboard, propelling Caleb with it.

The same strange, silent, floating sensation was followed by a ringing in his ears. Then there was a *thud* as the cab shuddered to an abrupt halt.

Caleb breathed hard, inhaling an unmistakable pungent stench. "Ugh!" he coughed. He opened his eyes cautiously to take in his surroundings. The cab's headlights shone upon a metal road sign. He never dreamt he'd be so overjoyed to read:

FETHERHAM SEWAGE PLANT.
NO ENTRY
TO UNAUTHORISED VEHICLES

HE'D DONE IT. HE WAS BACK.

Chapter Eight

Caleb's first instinct was to go to the bingo hall. The only way he could demonstrate his dad's innocence and save him from his unspeakable fate in this parallel world was to find Madame Zis and prove she was still alive. The bingo hall was where he last saw her.

It was late now and very dark. Fetherham town centre was back to its usual unkempt, deserted and poorly lit self. Caleb knew immediately that he was home. The only place open at this time of night was the kebab shop where a dull yellow light pulsed and flickered at the doorway and the toothless attendant sat alone at a table smoking. As he passed the old library, Caleb saw a woman sitting on the steps, surrounded by Piers Wooten-Maxwell and his gang. He slowed up to have a closer look and saw the distinctive green hat worn by Madame Zis. Yes, it was definitely her! She was clutching her handbag tightly to her chest while the group of boys taunted her.

"The thankless thug threatened to throttle his father," yelled one.

"The feathered thingummyjig thundered from the thorny thicket," added another.

"The thin thespian thought up a thrilling theory," piped up a third.

"Go on, say it!" cried Wooten-Maxwell, poking Madame Zis with his fencing foil.

With her strong Fezerham accent, the poor lady was getting in an awful muddle as she tried to repeat these phrases. Her hopeless attempts left the boys hugging their sides with uncontrollable laughter. Some had tears coursing down their cheeks. One was rolling on the ground shrieking, slapping the palm of his hand against the pavement.

Caleb set his jaw and tooted twice on his horn. Recognizing the taxi, Madame Zis stood up.

"It's the dog slayer!" one boy cried.

"Get in!" shouted Caleb to Madame Zis, who was clearly flustered.

"Zis taxi *again?*" he heard her wail, "Iz zis ze only taxi

around zese days?" She searched up and down the empty street as if looking for an alternative.

"It's this taxi or *them*!" called Caleb, nodding towards the gang, who were getting agitated.

"Odette Ocelot – get in this cab!" Caleb bellowed at the top of his voice.

Madame Zis scuttled down the library steps like a startled mouse and skittered round to the passenger side. No sooner was she inside than there was a thud as a cricket ball hit the bonnet. "Let's get out of here," hissed Caleb.

"Where are you taking me?" asked Madame Zis, her voice shrill with anxiety.

"Home – we need to talk," replied Caleb through gritted teeth. He glanced in the rear-view mirror. The gang was making threatening gestures towards the cab.

"Who are zose dreadful hooliganz?" Madame Zis asked, adjusting her hat and pulling her coat around her. "Zey dezerve a good flogging!"

"You're not supposed to hit children," replied Caleb. "It's against the law."

Madame Zis bristled with indignation. "But zey are

permitted to hit ze adults and jab zem wiz zere swords? Zat iz not against ze law?"

Caleb shook his head. "We are not where you think you are." It was so difficult to explain. "I mean to say, you have travelled far away from what you know as home."

Madame Zis looked at him blankly.

"I know it's difficult to take in, but you have somehow ended up here," Caleb continued. "I can take you back to where you come from, but you must agree to help me."

He stopped the cab. They were in front of his house. He peeled off his moustache and took off his flat cap, rubbing his hair.

"*Zut!* You are just a child!" exclaimed Madame Zis. She peered at him closely through narrowed eyes. "Why! You are zat same child zat drove out of ze bingo halle like a deranged lunatic earlier! You almost mowed all zose wretched people down! What are you doing dressed up like an old man and driving zis car, silly boy? Where are your parents?"

"Good question," said Caleb, reaching into his pocket and pulling out his wallet. He held it open and tapped the photograph of Bert Dallaway with his finger. "I think you might have already met my father."

"Ah! Ha ha!" cried Madame Zis, throwing her head back and clapping her hands together. "Well, zat explains everyzing." She pointed to the photo. "Zat man iz quite crazy." Then she pointed at Caleb. "And dogs don't make cats!"

Caleb had no idea what she meant and it showed in his face, but she continued regardless. "Your fazer zinks he knows about history. He has got it all wrong – he could not be more wrong!"

Caleb reached for the book that he'd taken out from the library. "Whereas you're the expert, right?"

"My book!" she gasped. She snatched it from Caleb and opened it, beaming with delight at its precious pages. "Where did you find zis?"

"I took it out of the library earlier."

"But ze library iz closed! I have been sitting zere for days – weeks. Zere iz never anyone coming to open it."

Caleb took the book and showed her the library stamp with today's date. "Not my library. *Your* library," he said.

"My library, your library," huffed Madame Zis. "What

are you talking about, imbecile boy?"

"There's another place, like this one but different," Caleb explained. "It's where you come from. There is a large town square, only it's nicer than the one here. There are families and children, cafés and shops. There are trams, airships… A place where everyone speaks the same as you."

"But zey have all *gone!*" she wailed, her hands falling into her lap in despair.

Caleb breathed slowly, summoning all his patience against the desire to throttle her. "I know it must be very strange for you," he said. "I feel exactly the same. But we have to work out what's happened. When did you start to notice the difference?"

She paused for a moment. "After ze accident," she said.

"Go on," urged Caleb.

"Ze one wiz zat silly fazer of yours." She jerked her head towards the photo. "He didn't see ze tram coming and swerved to miss it. Zen, *hup!*" She gave a little jolt. "Zuddenly I don't recognize anyzing any more."

Caleb thought back to the trams he'd seen in Fezerham. "Where did the accident happen?"

"Next to ze station. I waz on my way to visit my sister. She will be waiting for me!" She wrung her hands anxiously.

Caleb sighed. Everything was beginning to make more sense. His father's empty cab had been discovered by the station the day he went missing. It wasn't yet clear how Bert had found himself in Fezerham, or indeed why he was taking fares there. He certainly had never mentioned it to Caleb. But somehow he had got left behind while Madame Zis had switched worlds along with the cab.

"Do you know what happened to him? Where he went?" asked Caleb.

Madame Zis rubbed her temples. "I don't remember zat well," she said. "I received a blow to my head. I zink he waz ejected from ze car ... or he jumped. I'm really not sure."

"Let's go inside," said Caleb. "You can stay here tonight and I will take you home tomorrow. My father is in big trouble and only you can help him."

"What sort of trouble?" asked Madame Zis suspiciously. "How do you expect me to help you?"

"Where you come from, people believed he murdered you."

"Ha!" cried Madame Zis. The idea seemed to amuse her.

"It's not *funny*," said Caleb, feeling cross again. "He's in custody and will be guillotined unless I take you back and prove his innocence. You *must* trust me!"

"Well, if he iz a murderer zen ze guillotine iz what he dezerves!"

"But he's NOT a murderer!" Caleb's voice was shrill with frustration. "You're HERE! I'm talking to you – you're not DEAD!"

"Of course I'm not dead, idiot boy! I am sick – zat's what I am! Yes, sick with worry and confusion—"

"So trust me to take you back. Keep calm and leave things to me. Will you do that?"

Madame Zis exhaled loudly, whistling through her nose a little as she did so. "Finally perhapz zis iz not so complicated," she said, shrugging her shoulders. "I have been here for so long and just want to go home. You need me to help you to rescue your fazer, so you will take me back. It iz an everybody-win situation, *non?*"

"*Yes!*" agreed Caleb. It came out more as a sigh of relief than an actual word. For the first time he felt he was making some progress. "Now let's go inside," he continued. He needed to be careful not to upset the delicate sense of confidence that he had inspired in her. "It's late and we're both exhausted. There's nothing we can do right now. Best we get some sleep and leave first thing tomorrow."

He drove the cab into the garage, got out and shut the garage door behind them. Only then did he turn the light on and let Madame Zis out of the passenger side. "This is my father's workshop," he said, leading her to the room at the back of the garage. He unfolded the sofa bed, opened a cupboard that contained a duvet and a pillow, and set about making up the bed.

Madame Zis looked around her and sniffed the air like a wary animal.

"There're drinks in the fridge – you can help yourself. Also there are packets of soup in the cupboard if you get hungry ... and a kettle next to the sink. You must know how to use one of those. I'll lock you in – just so you feel safe – and bring you breakfast in the morning. It's very important that you must not try to leave this room. Do you understand? My mum will go spare if she knows there's an

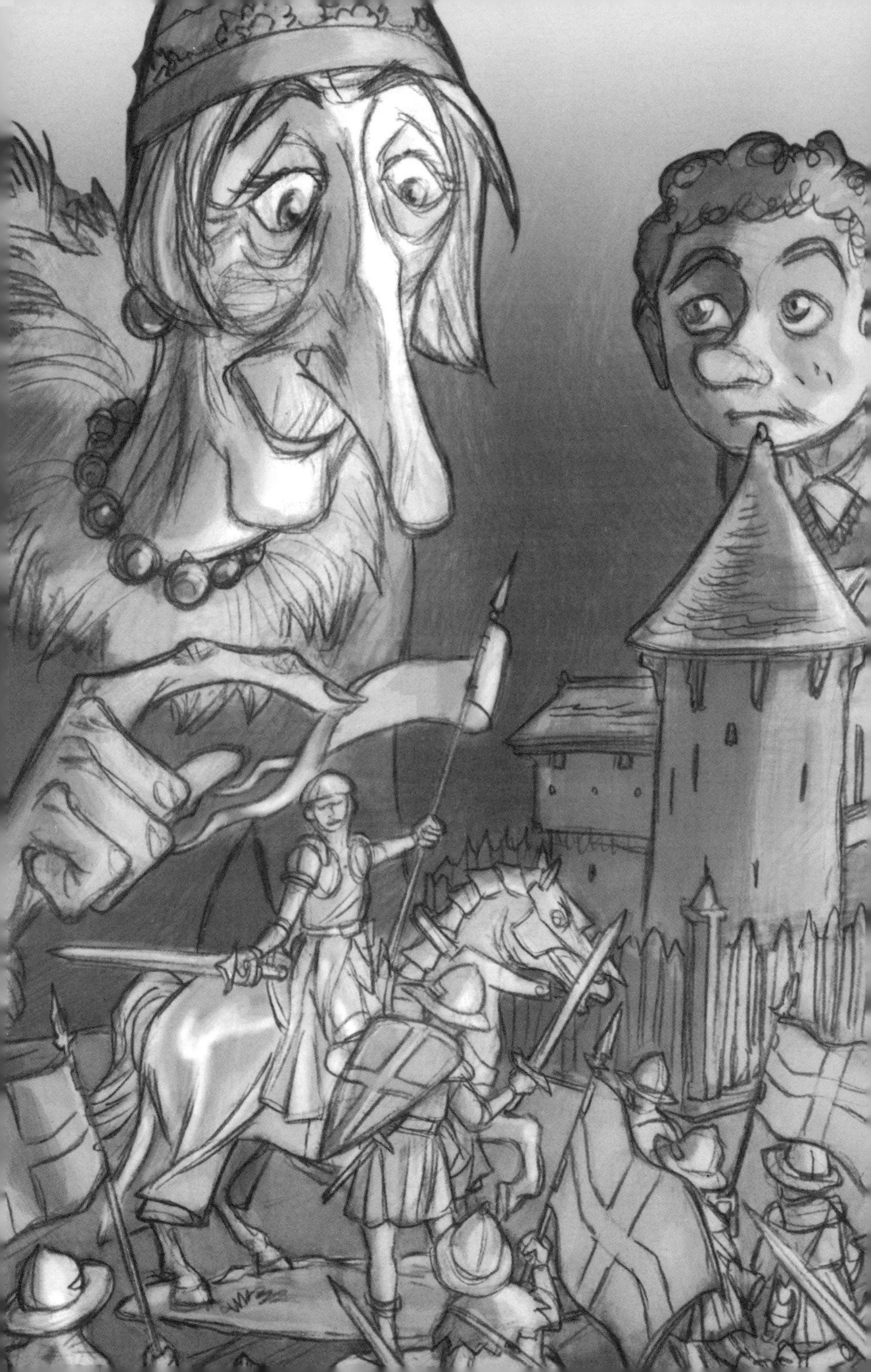

old person staying. She'll most likely call the police and then we'll be in an even worse muddle."

Madame Ziz didn't respond. Caleb turned round and saw her peering over the large table where Bert staged his battle reenactments. Her brow was knitted and she was tutting quietly to herself, picking up the miniature soldiers and rearranging them.

"But no wonder your fazer iz confused about hiz historical facts." She shook her head slightly. "He muddles hiz battles look here ..." She repositioned a few more soldiers. "Zere! Zat waz ze outcome of zis one." She held her palms out over the battlefield.

"But Dad's an expert on this sort of thing." Caleb sat on the bed and rubbed his hair. "He's lectured at universities and everything..."

Madame Zis looked at him and shook her head in disbelief.

"What is the name of where you live?" asked Caleb suddenly.

"Fezerham," mumbled Madame Zis, turning back to the table of figures.

"No, I mean the *country*. What country are you from?"

"Franzingland. Ze United Kingdoms of Franzingland!" She blinked at him. "And you?"

Caleb looked straight at her. "England," he said simply.

"But *England* iz consigned to ze history books. It iz a *medieval* country…"

Caleb shook his head. "But do you think that our histories could be different?" he asked slowly, hardly trusting his own theory. "Is that why our worlds are so contradictory?"

"Young man, ze older I get, the less I understand about most zings." She paused. "Why does your fazer create his soldiers in such valuable materials?" She held a solider up to the light. "Zis iz so extravagant! Aren't you afraid of burglars?"

"What is it with you lot and these soldiers?" Caleb snapped impatiently. "They're just tin!"

"Precisely! Zere iz a small fortune on zis table."

Caleb reached into his pocket and pulled out the coin he'd kept from earlier.

"So what's this made of?"

"Uh – why zat's nozing but gold," said Madame Zis, waving a hand dismissively.

Caleb closed his hand round the coin and put it back in his pocket. He remembered the busker on the steps of the library and the dozen or so coins in his instrument case. He grinned to himself. He'd had an idea. "Things are going to turn out just right for all of us – you'll see! Now, will you be all right?" he said.

"Yes. Go, go," she said wearily. "I am tired. I will wait for you in ze morning."

"You trust me?"

She shrugged. "I have no choice."

Caleb climbed the steps back up to the front door. Despite the evening's events, a knot of excitement had formed in his stomach. Not only was he going to be able to return Madame Zis to where she came from and be reunited with his father, but while he was in Franzingland, maybe he could also exchange some of his father's tin soldiers for enough gold coins to pay off the family's debts – a sort of inter-historical trade. His chest swelled with pleasure.

The house was quiet and in darkness, meaning Mopsy was still out with Measles. Caleb was used to an empty house, and having Mopsy out of the way was normally a good thing. On his way down the hallway, however, he noticed a faint glow from the lounge. Pushing open the door, he saw Mopsy sitting bolt upright in an armchair. She was staring straight ahead, her mouth drawn tight.

"Mum!" said Caleb, running to her and grasping her hands. "You wouldn't believe what happened to me tonight. It's just too weird for words … but I know where Dad is! He's in a spot of trouble, but I can help him … and, Mum, I think I've found the solution to all our debts…" He shook her shoulder. "Mum, *listen!*"

Mopsy remained motionless. Suddenly Caleb felt a firm grip at the top of his arm. A large hand clad in a black leather glove clasped his bicep. It hurt a little. He looked up and saw a scarred, square face belonging to a giant of a man. He looked back at Mopsy.

"I'm so sorry, Caleb," she wailed, her voice a whine. She dropped her head into her hands and began to sob. Caleb could smell the unmistakable tang of wine on her breath.

At that moment Measles stepped out of the shadows. He was smiling and holding a piece of paper. When Measles

smiled he looked like a colicky baby. He held the paper up
for Caleb to read.

C.A.S.H.
ACQUISITION
AGREEMENT FORM

Mopsy Dallaway

The room swirled. With sickening clarity Caleb realized
what he was looking at. His eyes scanned the page, finally
focusing at the bottom, where in girlish, scribbly writing,
was Mopsy's signature.

Chapter Nine

REF: DALLAWAY01
CHECKED BY: #245
RECOMMENDED SURVEILLANCE LEVEL - 1

Dear Mum,

I have just been told we are allowed to write home – so here's a letter.

Life here is repetitive and stuffed with pointless rules. General Tutoring takes place five hours a day and then we get split into specialized groups according to our "P.P.s" or Personal Profiles. My P.P. is still being assessed. I have to fill in pages and pages of multiple choice questions on how I would react to certain sets of circumstances. Here's an example:

If your house was on fire and your cat was locked in the bathroom, would you:

a) kick down the blazing bathroom door and save the cat before escaping to safety;

b) get out of your blazing house as fast as you could and tell the firemen the cat needed rescuing;

c) forget the cat and save the family silverware from the sideboard;

d) get out of your blazing house as fast as you could and instruct the firemen that the silverware must be rescued from the sideboard.

When I've finished answering all these – and there are literally hundreds of them – my responses will get analyzed by a computer and my group designated according to the results. The possible groups are C.A.S.H. Acquisitions, Traders, Brokers, Investments, Sales, Debt Recuperation, Accountants, Bookkeepers or Cashiers. They all sound thrilling, don't they?

The only good thing that's happened since I arrived is that I've found Myra – but she's not the same. She seems to have gone a bit stupid in the head. She's all gormless and dopey – not at all her usual fiery self. I'll have to get to the bottom of it as maybe she is homesick and just doesn't want to talk. I am told many children are traumatized by the act of betrayal. I hope you are feeling guilty! How is life now it's debt free? Write soon.

Caleb

Darling Caleb,

How lovely to get your letter. Yes, I do feel so horribly guilty, and life at home is miserable without you. When you next write, you must send me some of the recipes you used to cook for us, like that delicious spam curry. I am struggling a bit in the kitchen and if I carry on eating out at restaurants all the time I am going to get hideously fat. I'll need some tips for supermarket shopping too – like, how do you separate one trolley from another? They all seem to be chained up together!

On another note, I am a bit puzzled by some of the noises coming from the garage since you've gone. I wonder if you inadvertently shut a fox in when you closed it last? There's a lot of shuffling going on down there – especially at night. I wish you were here to go down and check it out. I'm petrified of foxes.

Have you got your group assigned yet?

Write soon.

Mum x

Dear Mum,

If there is a fox in the garage, my advice is to just let it be, and above all don't go down there as they can be very vicious, especially in confined places. It is likely to leap at your throat if you disturb it.

Aren't you the lucky one eating out at restaurants! The food here is mostly vile, although oddly enough we are allowed Smarties at breakfast which are a welcome respite from the slop we get at other mealtimes. They're about the only thing I can stomach here – thank god for the Smarties – I'd starve without them!

Myra continues to confuse me. She blanks me whenever I talk to her – very odd. It's like she's been brainwashed. In fact most of the kids here act like zombies. Maybe that's what reading The Money Mongers Encyclopaedia of Advanced Economics does to you! I've just been given a copy to read for a test next week. I can barely lift it, it's so heavy. I will start my training for the cash machines tomorrow. There's a script I need to learn. Meantime, your friend Mr Measles has decided to liven things up a bit by announcing a "Design a Tie" competition – "just for fun" the memo said.

Honestly, Mum, what do you see in him?

Caleb

Dear Caleb,

You know, I'm not sure it's a fox after all — unless foxes have evolved to hum tunes. No, really — I distinctly heard humming coming from the garage the other morning. I'm so worried. What if I have a squatter downstairs? I'm a sitting duck, Caleb! What should I do? Please write by return. I'm scared...

Mum x

REF: DALLAWAY01
CHECKED BY: #475
RECOMMENDED SURVEILLANCE LEVEL - 1

Dear Mum,

It's important you don't go down into the workshop as I reckon your first hunch that it's a wild animal is spot on. Are you sure it was humming you heard? Perhaps it was some sort of whining? Perhaps you are becoming a bit hysterical? It seems that living on your own is not suiting you at all — but you should have thought of that before you did the deal with Measles!

I have been grouped in Investments but am borderline Broker so am under observation in case they decide to move me up a group. I fell short on the qualities required of a Trader (a fact of which

I am secretly proud). I am progressing with my cash-machine training and have almost all my script learned by heart. I should be allowed to "couple" (i.e. sit with someone else) in a live session with the public next week. They put us newbies with a chaperone for each session – an older boy or girl who breathes down your neck and makes sure you don't screw it up.

I am feeling rather unwell these days, like my head is stuffed with cotton wool. I have been refused a medical consultation – they say it's all part of the normal adjustment period.

Caleb

Dearest Caleb

It's worse than I thought.

I saw it – or should I say her! It's a woman – and she's ... oh, good God, Caleb, I can hardly bear to write it. She's OLD! Positively geriatric! There is a grey-haired veteran tottering around in my garage!!! I am scared rigid. You know what old people are like – half mad, half dead. She should be in a home of some sort, surely. What should I do? Call the police? I will wait for your instructions but PLEASE, PLEASE, HURRY!

Mum x

Mum,

PLEASE DO NOT PANIC!

The truth is, I know who it is in the workshop and she poses no threat to you. On the contrary, she holds the key to getting our life back on track – so, please, please, do not do anything rash. It may shock you to learn that she is there by my invitation. That was what I was trying to tell you the night Measles took me away. I'm not sure if my letters are secure so I can't go into detail, but, trust me, you must not UNDER ANY CIRCUMSTANCES let this lady leave! If you scare her away, we are doomed. I can't tell you more – but please trust me. I will be there to sort out the situation very soon.

Caleb

Caleb!

You seem to have gone quite insane. I cannot bear the idea of this old woman living in the workshop and I refuse to believe that she is as important as you say she is. What can she possibly do for us? Unless you can give me a sensible reason why I should not get this woman forcefully evicted, I will have no choice but to call the authorities. I give you the return of mail to convince me.

Mum x

P.S. What can you mean when you say "I'll be there to sort out the situation"? You are institutionalized, Caleb – they will not allow you to leave! Sorry to be so blunt, but it's how things are…

REF: DALLAWAY01
CHECKED BY: #443
REFER TO MEASLES - **HIGH ALERT**

Dear Mum,

For security reasons, I am reluctant to write so candidly, but your failure to trust me leaves me no choice. This revelation in itself could jeopardize everything.

The night Measles took me away I was trying to explain something to you. Something very, very important…

Caleb was still feeling unwell. His head ached and he was finding it difficult to focus on the complicated story of his discovery of Franzingland. But he was between a rock and a hard place. If he didn't come clean to his mother, who was clearly panicking and likely to do something impulsive, he could lose Madame Zis and his dad would be doomed.

He'd started his letter in G.R. (General Recreation) and continued after supper during C.P. (Consolidation Period) while he was supposed to be learning his script for the cash machine. He finished the letter by the light of a torch underneath his bed covers while the other boys in his dormitory were sleeping.

So you see? That's what I was trying to tell you the night I was taken away, and that's why it's so very important you don't evict Madame Zis. I will be home as soon as I can, although God knows how because this place is like Fort Knox — but I will find a way and fast. Sit tight and wait for me.

Caleb rubbed his eyes. It was very late. His writing hand ached and his eyes felt dry and stabby, but he was relieved it was done. He folded the letter and put it in an envelope before slipping silently out of bed and posting it in the dormitory postbox.

The letter would never reach Mopsy.

First thing the next morning, one of the correspondence monitors opened it, stamped it with a high-alert surveillance warning and delivered it to Measles's office, marked for his urgent attention.

Chapter Ten

Caleb's heart was rock heavy. It was just over two weeks since he'd been admitted to the Money Mongers's custody and life here was grim. There was none of the jostling and excited chatter of a real school. The children mooched about zombie-like, with pale, pinched little faces and tight little mouths.

In the stark, grey canteen, Caleb sat down next to Myra for their mid-morning snack. He placed his bag of books down on the pale yellow-and-green linoleum floor beside their bench. They were sitting slightly apart from the other children and, taking advantage of the relative intimacy, Caleb tried once more to talk to his friend. "Myra," he said softly, nudging her with his elbow, "how are we going to get out of here?"

"We can't," she said coldly, looking straight ahead and munching noisily on a plain digestive. Even the biscuits were boring.

"But I *need* to get out," Caleb persisted. "Dad's in deep trouble. Myra, I wish I could talk to you about it…"

"Things are different now, Caleb," she said, wearing the same blank face and speaking in the same monotone voice.

"Ah – so you admit you've changed then?" ventured Caleb. "I don't understand you, Myra. We used to have so much fun together, don't you remember?"

"Fun has no place here," she replied, this time looking at him. "Fun gets left at the door as soon as you set foot inside, along with other stuff like friendship and hope." She paused to brush some crumbs off her skirt. Caleb pushed his bottom lip out and looked at the ground. Myra breathed in hard and continued. "You just don't get it, do you? Our parents have given us away for money. They sold us. What *fun* can be had after that?" She looked away again, pushing a straw into a carton of milk and sucking half-heartedly at it. "Even if we did get out, where would we go? We're clearly not wanted at home..."

Caleb was unable to conceal his dismay. This was the most Myra had spoken to him since his arrival but it was hardly the breakthrough he'd hoped for. What was with all the morose defeatism? It simply wasn't the Myra he had so desperately missed all these months. As they sat in awkward silence, Caleb wracked his brains for something clever to say that would snap her out of it. Then a bell rang, prompting her to gather up her things and stand up. She tossed her milk carton into the bin and slouched out of the canteen without a word.

Caleb's head ached and his brain felt fuzzy as he made his way to Cash Machine Training. Even learning the simple lines for his first "live" session with the public had taken a massive effort. He still wasn't confident he knew his script by heart.

As he walked into the classroom he saw a cash-machine simulator had been set up. There was a small chair behind a desk with a drawer full of bank notes. On the desk was a cash-machine computer and a microphone. Other than lacking a one-way mirror and thick, reinforced walls, the simulator was just like the real thing.

Caleb slipped into the chair, knowing it was his turn to start first, and waited for the class monitor to arrive.

Eventually a stocky, round woman with curly, short hair entered the room. She wore a grey suit and a pale-pink cashmere sweater with matching pearls around her fat neck. Her feet were stuffed into navy court shoes, which made a *tap tap* noise as she walked. Caleb couldn't help thinking she was the ugliest woman he'd ever seen.

"Good morning, class," she snapped, without smiling.

"Good morning, Monitor Trotter," the class droned in reply.

"Dallaway – we'll start without delay," she continued. "I hope you've learned your script." She placed herself before the simulator.

Caleb shifted slightly in his chair and cleared his throat. "Good morning, Madam," he began. "I'm your C.A.S.H. provider today. Please insert your card."

Monitor Trotter pounced on his first mistake with what seemed like glee. "Dismal start, Dallaway! You forgot the word *happy*! Start again!"

"Good morning, Madam," Caleb repeated. "I'm your *happy* C.A.S.H. provider today. Please insert your card."

Trotter halted the role play and turned to address the class. "Can someone tell me why the word 'happy' is so important?"

"Service with a smile?" ventured someone towards the back of the room.

"Almost … but not quite. Anyone else?"

The room was silent. Monitor Trotter took a sharp intake of air. "The word 'happy' is vital because the happier you sound, the more likely people are to use the cash machine and make the bank money – clear?"

A few of the children nodded and Trotter returned her attention to the simulator. She entered a card and some virtual bank account information, which was displayed on the screen next to Caleb.

"Thank you. Now enter the amount required," he said.

Trotter typed in a large sum of money with her podgy fingers.

"One moment. I am pleased to be dealing with your request." Caleb counted out the money and slipped it towards the imaginary hatch. "Please take your cash. Don't forget your bankcard. Have a nice day, it has been a pleasure serving you."

"*No, no, NO!*" Trotter screeched, her face turning an unusually dark shade of pink. "It's just not *POSSIBLE!*"

Caleb looked at her, confused. The sign-off was the only part of the script he was sure of.

"Look at your screen!" she barked. "How much money do I have in my account?"

Caleb studied the screen again and gulped. "Er, you don't have the funds…" he stammered.

"And yet you have dispensed them anyway! You have

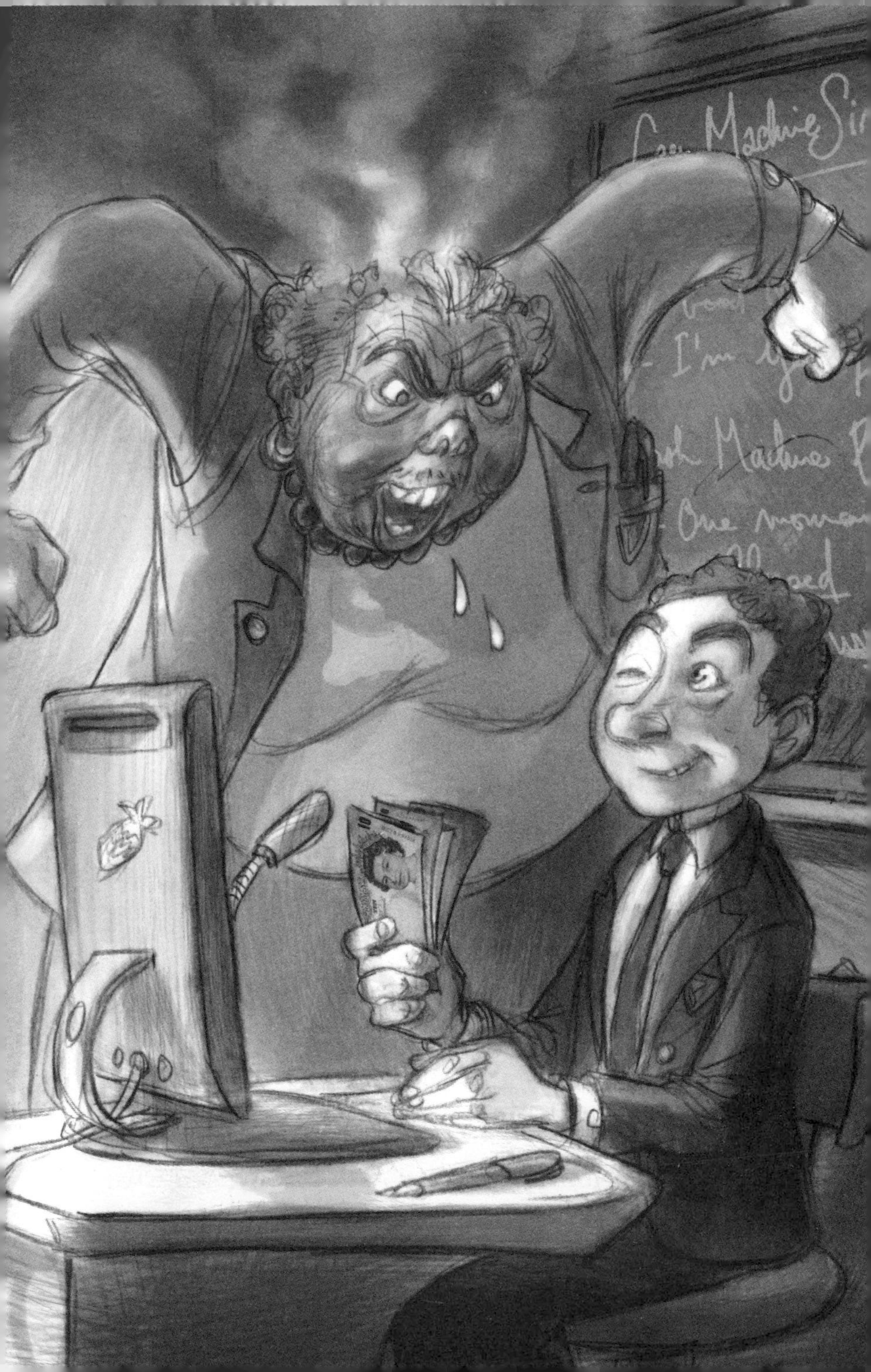

broken the golden rule! Your mindless action has *lost us money!*" Monitor Trotter's voice was becoming more and more shrill and her beady eyes bulged furiously. Caleb felt an involuntary smirk sneaking up around his lips.

"And you think this is funny?" she squawked.

"Not at all," replied Caleb. Then before he could stop himself, he added, "I think *you* are funny—"

Monitor Trotter's hands flew to her hips. She wore several rings that cut into her plump, sausage-like fingers. "And, tell me, are you planning to make fun of everyone who visits our cash machines?"

"I wasn't making fun," explained Caleb. "I just smiled a bit. No one would be able to see that anyway."

"It is *un-pro-fessional*," sniped Trotter, pushing her round face up to Caleb's. He held his breath against the smell of stale coffee coming from her chubby lips. "Any manner of facial expression will be detected in your voice. You must remain expressionless at all times ... do you understand?"

"But—"

"DO YOU UNDERSTAND?"

"Yes," murmured Caleb.

"I beg your pardon?"

"YES!" Caleb bawled, staring her straight in the eye. All of a sudden, he'd lost the urge to laugh. Instead he felt incensed.

There was a stunned silence as Caleb and Monitor Trotter eyeballed one another, their faces almost touching. Then Trotter drew herself up, looking at him through narrowed eyes. She scribbled on her clipboard:

Dallaway — tendency for impulsivity not overcome. Prescribe increased dose of Monointuniv 20. Effective immediately.

Then she smiled sourly. "Now, let's start again from where you went wrong, Dallaway. Repeat the protocol for Insufficient Funds…"

The lesson dragged on for another excruciating hour. Caleb's temples throbbed more with each passing minute. When the bell went at midday he could hardly contain his relief.

Back in the canteen, lunch was a flavourless spinach and turnip soup, followed by potted meat with boiled potatoes and some sort of sloppy yogurt, which had clearly been watered down to make it stretch further. The children ate without talking, seated along long rows of trestle tables. Myra and Caleb sat together in silence. As Caleb sipped his soup, he caught a glimpse of Measles talking to Monitor Trotter. It was not a good sign. Measles rarely showed up unless there was something urgent. Trotter was showing him her clipboard. Measles nodded and looked up in Caleb's direction. His face was set and severe. Then to Caleb's dismay, Measles pointed a bony finger in his direction and signalled for him to come over. Caleb swallowed his mouthful, stood slowly and made his way towards them.

"Dallaway, I am led to understand you're having some issues with *fitting in*," Measles said, spluttering slightly over the word "fitting".

"No, sir," replied Caleb, his eyes fixed on the bubble of spit that had settled on Measles's lower lip.

Measles ignored his response. "Hardly surprising given your parents' profiles," he sneered. He held Trotter's clipboard in his hand. "Mother – unemployed and undereducated, with alcoholic tendencies," he read. "Father (absent) – socialist, taxi-driver, *historian*." He said the word *historian* as if it was some kind of vulgar, senseless pastime.

Caleb tried to glance round the edge of the clipboard to see what else had been written about him. Hearing Measles describe his mother like this when he had positively *flirted* with her over the past months just didn't make sense. Had it just been part of Measles's strategy to get her to sign him over to the Money Mongers?

Measles snapped the clipboard to his chest. "Come and see me first thing tomorrow morning. Knock three times on my office door and await my instructions." Then he clicked the heels of his shoes together before executing a perfect half-spin and marching away. Caleb watched him, seething with hatred.

"Back to your table, Dallaway!" called one of the monitors.

Caleb slumped back to his bench. He knew it was only a matter of days before – in another world entirely – his father was due to be executed. He repeated the word "executed" over and over in his head until he began to feel sick. Unable to swallow another bite of food, he pushed his bowl away and turned to Myra who had finished eating now and was examining her fingernails. He willed her to look up at him – just once. One smile from his best friend would help take the edge off his misery. But Myra's eyes remained fixed on her nails and for the first time since he had arrived, Caleb felt the fight drain out of him and the tears well up in his eyes.

Chapter Eleven

Caleb was in low spirits as he made his way from the washrooms back to the dorm that evening. The corridor, covered in the same boring linoleum as the canteen, was long and dimly lit. The other children were already in bed and everywhere was deadly silent. Caleb dragged his feet, breathing in the acrid smell of detergent that had been used to mop the floors when suddenly he felt a violent tug on his pyjama collar, and found himself being yanked sideways into a caretaker's cupboard.

The door slammed shut. A torchlight flicked on, and to his surprise and delight he saw Myra! Her eyes were bright and flashing, just like they used to be, full of intelligence and spirit. She was wearing a long flannel nightdress. Her face was scrubbed and shiny.

"Caleb, it's me!" she hissed.

Instantly he knew what she meant. Of course it was her

– but this time it was the real Myra, *his* Myra.

"What's going on, My? You frightened the life out of me!"

"Caleb, you must believe me ... they are *drugging* us."

"What are you talking about? Slow down!"

"Listen. You've been feeling unwell, right? Dizzy, tired, headachy? And I bet you're finding it hard to concentrate?"

Caleb was feeling all those things right now. Perhaps it was the shock of this encounter? "Yes!" he blurted.

Myra signalled to him to hush. She continued in an urgent whisper, "At breakfast when they give you that pot of Smarties – well, they're not ... they're not Smarties – at least not the red ones. You see, there are always two red ones in each pot – I've worked it all out. The red ones are disguised. They are sort of *will-sapping* drugs, Caleb. They give them to us to keep us quiet – to make us forget, so we don't question what's going on. Don't ever, ever eat the red ones!"

Caleb had been eating the Smarties eagerly – they were the only treat on offer in this ghastly place. He felt confused. "But you're OK," he said, "at least you are tonight. Up till now, you've been so *different*."

"I've been *pretending* to be sick!" she said, slowly

123

pronouncing each syllable. "I worked out what they were up to a long time ago. I've been stashing my drugs ever since – they're part of my escape plan." Her eyes danced mischievously in the torchlight.

"Escape? B-but how?" he stammered. "This place is like a prison. We're locked in permanently, with chaperones and cameras watching us twenty-four seven. There's never a moment without somebody or something spying on us! Oh, Myra, if only you knew how important it is I get out of here – *and soon...*"

"*I know!* Why else would I bother dragging you into the cupboard, you moron? We'll do it together, but you have to listen – very carefully."

Caleb nodded.

"Tomorrow I'm on cash machine duty – the late shift from seven to ten."

Caleb nodded again.

"You need to find a way to come and join me at eight thirty sharp because that's when we're blasting out of here."

"But your chaperone?" he asked. "There's no way I'd get past them unnoticed."

"Don't worry. It's all part of my plan. I'm going to give my chaperone my stash of Monointuniv 20."

What is she talking about, Caleb puzzled.

"The *red Smarties!*" hissed Myra. "I've got tons of them saved up – enough to knock out a rhinoceros. I'll put them in his flask and they'll dope him up for hours!"

"But *how…*" Caleb was still unsure. Had Myra got her hands on some explosives? How on earth was she going to blast her way out?

But before he could get any more information out of her, they heard footsteps. Myra switched off her torch immediately. "Go, Caleb," she whispered. "Just trust me… Be at the machine at eight thirty sharp. OK?"

Caleb nodded, not the best response in the pitch dark of the cupboard.

"OK, Caleb?" she asked, more urgently.

"Yes, of course. I'll be there."

Chapter Twelve

aleb hardly slept a wink that night. He lay in bed and pinched himself at regular intervals to make sure he wasn't dreaming. He wasn't at all convinced he hadn't hallucinated the entire episode in the cupboard with Myra. Neither was he reassured at breakfast. She didn't look his way even once. It left him doubly uncertain of the plan they had hatched. Her gormless expression had returned and Caleb watched in dismay as she shovelled cereal into her mouth, her eyes blank and her shoulders slumped.

As usual the monitors came round with the pots of multi-coloured "Smarties", plonking them down on the tables as if they were dispensing them to livestock. They were the nearest anyone got to eating sweets in C.A.S.H. custody, and Caleb watched the other children gobble them down greedily. This time he noticed he'd been given three red ones, instead of two. If what Myra had said was true, then someone wanted to keep him especially quiet. Although he felt unsure of everything Myra had revealed the night before, he avoided eating them, sliding them into his pocket when no one was looking.

After breakfast, instead of heading for lessons, Caleb went to Measles's office as instructed. He knocked three times and waited. Behind the door he heard the sound of shuffling, a scraping chair and the sliding of drawers. This went on for several moments and Caleb was just about to knock again when a voice called out, "Enter."

He opened the door and walked in. Measles was standing by a mirror, smoothing his hair with his bony hand – the exact same gesture Caleb had seen him perform when he'd visited his mum. *Did she have any idea*, he wondered, *what was going on here?* He doubted it.

"Sit," said Measles, turning and glaring at him coldly.

Caleb did as he was told.

Measles's office was predictably austere. There were no knick-knacks or photos of loved ones, no scribbly drawings saying "I love Daddy" pinned on the walls. In fact there was no evidence of a life outside the bank at all. Instead there was a vast wall of television screens, each transmitting stilted images from the many CCTV cameras installed throughout the building. It was clear Measles was spying on everyone every minute of the day. It made Caleb shudder.

Without saying a word, Measles opened a drawer and pulled out a plump envelope, which had Caleb's handwriting on it. He recognized instantly that Measles was holding the last, crucial letter he had written to his mother.

Measles switched on his desk light and adjusted the head so it shone directly in Caleb's face. "You have a very fertile imagination, young man," he said, fingering the envelope. "Do you want to tell me more about the contents of this missive?"

Caleb shuffled uncomfortably in his seat, squinting against the bright light of the bulb. Behind it, Measles was little more than a creepy silhouette.

"No – not really. Like you say – it's all made up…"

"*All* made up?" repeated Measles, with more than a hint of sarcasm. "How very disappointing… Even the bit about all that lovely *gold*? If you know of a place where there is an unlimited supply of gold, you know it is your duty to tell me all about it – even to take me there. You understand that, don't you, Caleb?"

Caleb nodded. "Really, it's – it's all fabricated," he stammered. "I had a hunch our letters were being intercepted. I wrote all that stuff to see if I was right."

Measles's fist tightened, scrunching up the letter. "You're not doing well here, Dallaway," he growled through clenched jaws. "Not well at all." He stood up and started to pace to and fro behind his desk. "Monitor Trotter was bitterly disappointed with your attitude yesterday and she is quite alarmed by the security threat you pose. She describes you as cocky … *arrogant* even… " Still clutching Caleb's letter, Measles leaned both fists on his desk and bent closer. "You seem to think yourself *special*, Dallaway. An *individual*. *Different* from all the others." He emphasized each word for effect. "Is that a fair analysis?"

"Not really, sir," replied Caleb glumly.

"I hope not, for your sake, Dallaway…"

There was a pause while Measles took something from round his neck. With the bright light still shining in his eyes,

Caleb couldn't be sure what it was until Measles plonked a laminated card on the desk in front of him. It was a three-dimensional hologram featuring a sequence of squiggly lines and dots.

"Do you know what this is, Dallaway?"

"No, sir," replied Caleb, squirming.

"It is a hi-tech image of a DNA profile, Dallaway. My DNA profile. This allows me, and only me, to access every nook and cranny of this bank, from the vaults and safes to the washrooms. This, Dallaway..." he tapped his slender finger on the pattern of lines and dots, "is the single expression of *individuality* that is permitted by this bank. Do you see what I am driving at?"

"I think so," replied Caleb, feeling his forehead prickle with sweat.

"Well, just in case things are still a little obscure, let me make myself clear." He snatched his identity card up from the desk and put it back round his neck. "Outside correspondence will be forbidden from now on – no letters or communication of any kind with your family. Is that understood?"

Caleb nodded.

"I'm allowing you some time to curb your imagination – or indeed to confess to what you know." He waved the crumpled letter in Caleb's direction. "This matter is far from closed. Far from closed…" Measles whipped open his desk drawer, threw the letter in and slammed it shut. Then he drew himself up to his full height. "I will arrange for another … interview … in the coming days. In the meantime, know that I am watching you, Dallaway. I am watching you very closely. *Now get out of my office!*"

Caleb hurriedly got up from his seat and skittered to the door. As he reached for the handle, Measles spoke up once more, his voice icy and menacing. "I always get what I want, Dallaway. The sooner you come to terms with that the better. Come hell or high water – I always get what I want…"

Caleb felt a chill slide down his spine. As he stumbled along the corridor, his mind was racing. If his mum hadn't received his letter then she had probably kicked Madame Zis out of the house by now. He wasn't sure he'd manage to get back to Franzingland in time, even if he and Myra were able to escape. And, worse, if he didn't have Madame Zis with him as proof of his dad's innocence, it was unlikely he'd pull off the rescue at all.

Chapter Thirteen

Over lunch Caleb once again searched Myra's face, desperate to get some signal from her that the conversation in the caretaker's cupboard had been real. But she remained aloof and distant and as Caleb left the canteen his heart was thumping despondently in his chest. The only way he'd know for sure if she had been serious would be to play along with her plan and meet her at eight thirty, like she'd said.

The rest of the day dragged interminably. Caleb went from one lesson to the next, willing the hands of the clock to move quicker. During C.P., he roughed out a sketch for the obligatory "design a tie" competition. He chose a blue-marine background with bars of gold stacked one above the other to spell the word "lovely". It was hideous, and bound to get him into trouble, but he submitted it anyway and then went to supper.

The time had almost come. Myra was nowhere to be seen. She must have already started her cash-machine session. Caleb's stomach flitted with butterflies and he could hardly bear to eat. Not wanting to draw attention to himself, he forced down his meal of corned beef fritters and yellowing broccoli, followed by a triangular portion of plasticky cheese and dry crackers. Afterwards he sat waiting while the other children wrote letters home.

Caleb needn't have worried. Myra's plan was going like clockwork. Her chaperone was a jittery, skinny youth with bitten nails and a pock-marked complexion. She couldn't even remember his name – and she knew he didn't know hers. When he needed to address her, he called her "Toots". He was more interested in making calls on his phone than keeping an eye on her, so while he was distracted, Myra unscrewed his flask of hot chocolate and tipped in several months' supply of Monointuniv 20. She replaced the screw top and shook the flask to make sure the tablets were well dissolved. Then she squeezed into the cash machine control pod and waited. Her chaperone sat outside the pod, sipping his hot chocolate and sending text messages. After about an hour, she heard the reassuring sound of snoring. The first phase of her plan was coming together.

Meanwhile, Caleb slipped out of the study room under the pretense of needing the toilet. Apprehensively he began to make his way to the unauthorized cash-machine sector of the building. Because of the cash-pods and the proximity of the outside world, security was tighter here than anywhere else and entering without permission courted hefty punishment. He padded softly down the dimly lit corridors unobserved.

Or so he thought.

Alone in his office, Measles was watching Caleb via the CCTV. The pages of Caleb's letter to his mother were scattered over his desk. As he followed Caleb's every move, his leather-gloved hand hovered above a red alarm button. If he pressed it, the security guards would swarm in, capture Caleb and bring him straight to the office. But for now his curiosity got the better of him and he was keen to know what Caleb would do next.

Myra's cash pod was easy to find and Caleb tiptoed carefully past the sleeping chaperone before knocking softly on the wall. She turned and smiled, immediately putting

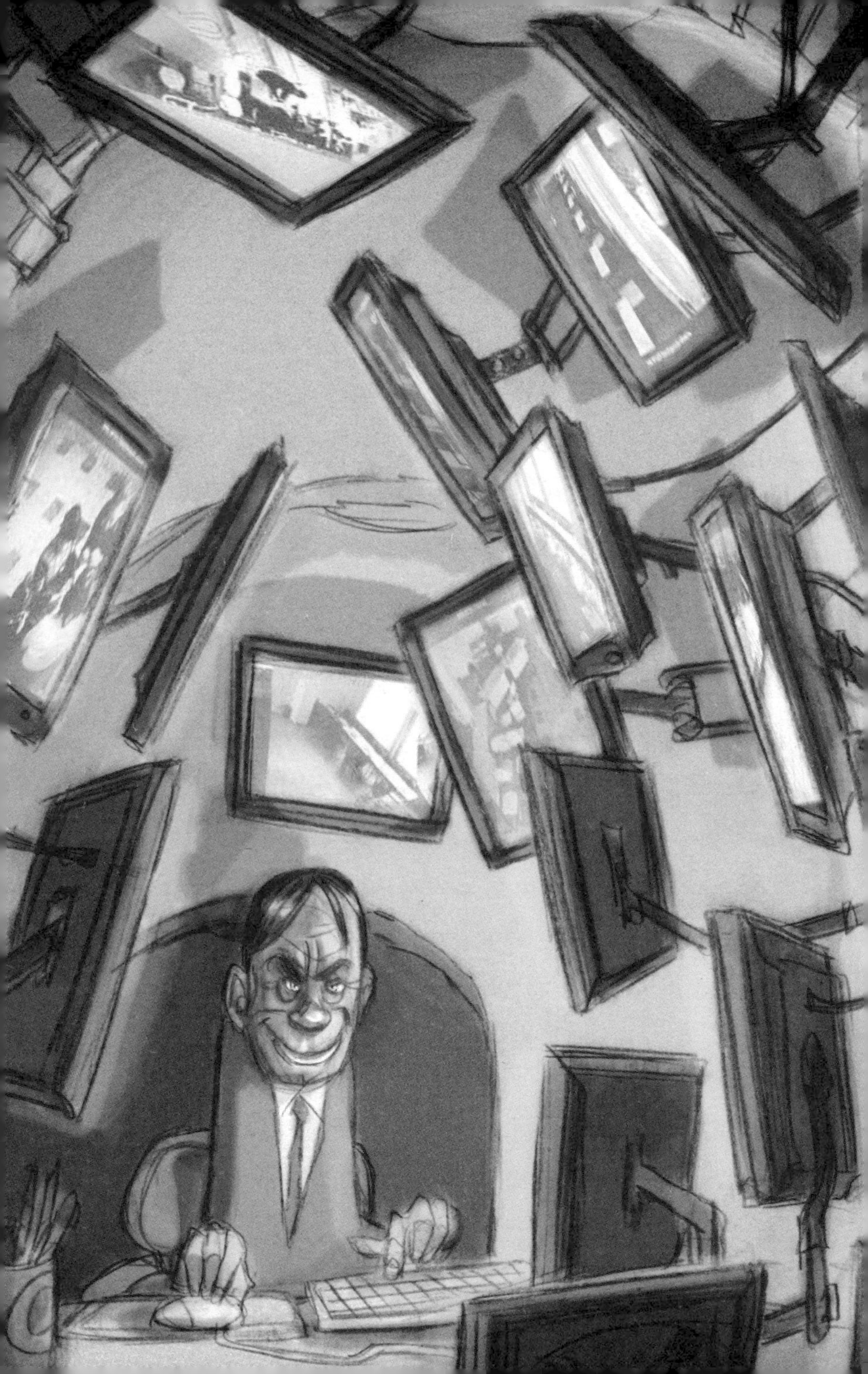

him at ease. "Just in time!" she mouthed, beckoning him to join her in the pod.

It was eight thirty.

Right on time, the stocky form of Piers Wooten-Maxwell, dressed in his jodhpurs and riding hat, trotted up to the cash machine on his horse, Snarls.

Snarls was a very expensive thoroughbred polo pony. He was highly strung and volatile, as over-indulged and temperamental as his owner. It was rumoured Piers fed him on fish fingers, because Snarls refused all normal horse food, and this unorthodox diet made him particularly aggressive. Snarls and Piers made a fearful team and Myra was determined to make best use of them.

Caleb and Myra watched as Piers jumped off Snarls' back and hooked the reins over his arm. The horse twitched and fidgeted, taking bad-tempered nips out of the brick wall surrounding the cash machine. Piers touched the screen, flipped open his wallet and waited while Myra began her script.

"Good evening, sir, I'm your happy cash provider today. Please insert your card."

Wooten-Maxwell inserted his card.

"Thank you," responded Myra, "and may I add what a complete twazzock you look this evening! Please enter the amount required."

"What?" roared Wooten-Maxwell.

Inwardly, Caleb was screaming the same word. What on earth was Myra doing?!

She winked at him and continued to speak. "Enter the amount required, numbnuts, or are you deaf as well as ugly?"

Wooten-Maxwell slammed his fist against the controls. "Bloody thing's broken!" he hissed under his breath.

"Who are you calling broken, you odious twonk? Just enter the amount you want and get lost. You're spoiling my evening with your sticking-out ears and smelly breath!"

Wooten-Maxwell reddened with rage. He hammered the amount into the keypad.

"Ha!" cried Myra, gleefully. "I do believe you have insufficient funds. I cannot authorize this transaction so I am going to have to keep your card. Have a nice day. It has been a pleasure serving you!"

"Give that card back!" barked Wooten-Maxwell.

"Come and get it!" retorted Myra.

"Why you—" began Wooten-Maxwell, thumping both fists on the cash dispenser.

"He's going to break right through," Myra hissed at Caleb. "That horse is bonkers – he'll use it to smash down the wall, you'll see…"

Caleb understood immediately. If Piers and his horse brought the wall down, they'd be able to make their escape. Myra was a genius.

Wooten-Maxwell continued to hurl insults at the machine while Snarls became more and more agitated, spinning and prancing as if spoiling for a fight. He pawed the ground with his front hoof, like an angry bull, before kicking out like a bucking bronco.

Caleb grabbed Myra's hand and they waited as the pod trembled with each hefty kick. After several minutes, however, Wooten Maxwell stopped his tirade and gave the machine a final thump. He remounted Snarls and cantered away. She slumped back in her chair.

Myra's expression turned from delight to despair. "Oh, no!" she breathed, turning off the microphone so she couldn't be heard outside. "Don't go! No, no, no, no! You're not supposed to go!"

The chaperone snorted and stirred before settling back into unconsciousness. Myra began to sob silently. Caleb knew Wooten-Maxwell was bound to complain and Myra would be disciplined severely – probably even locked up

in one of the institution's dreaded "taming-chambers". No one quite knew what went on in these chambers, but they were rumored to break the spirit of even the most stubborn children. They would realize she hadn't been taking her Monointuniv 20 and would find another way to drug her. She was doomed. Caleb sighed and squeezed her shoulder. He could offer no words of comfort – they both knew their last ounce of hope was drained.

It was ghostly silent. Caleb's hand rested limply on Myra's shoulder which shuddered up and down while she wept. The chaperone breathed heavily and rhythmically – the silence of defeat was unbearable.

Then suddenly, Caleb's grip on Myra's shoulder tightened. "What's that?" he whispered.

Myra heard it too. She looked up, her tear-stained face suddenly alert. Caleb gradually made out the sound of horses' hooves approaching. Myra sniffed and wiped her face with her sleeve. The clatter of hooves got louder. It soon became clear that there was more than one horse this time – perhaps three or four – a veritable cavalry.

"It's him! Ha-ha!" Myra clapped her hands. "It's him,

Caleb! And he's brought the gang! Oh, this is better than I thought! Brace yourself!"

She switched the microphone back on. "So you're back, mug-muppet!" she yelled. "With that sorry excuse of a nag. When's its appointment with the glue factory?"

"That's the one!" screamed Wooten-Maxwell, pointing at the cash machine with his riding crop. *"Charge!"*

The boys from the polo club whipped and shouted at their horses, working the startled beasts into a frenzy. Led by Snarls, who was foaming at the mouth, the horses reared and kicked out at the insolent cash machine, gradually pulverizing the brickwork around it. Myra pressed herself to the back of the cash pod, frightened but exhilarated, as the reinforced wall buckled under the hammering of the horses' hooves. "Get ready, Caleb," she said, holding out her hand to him. As he took it, she spoke once more into the microphone. "Your parents are almost bankrupt anyway, *Wooden-Cracksmell!* It's pointless breaking in; the Money Mongers will soon be marching you in through the front door..."

Her words were drowned out by a hoof crashing through the steel casing, ripping out a large chunk of wall. The cash machine's live wires tangled around one of the horse's legs, and sparkled and fizzed like a firework. The terrified animal bolted in panic.

"Bingo, let's go!" cried Myra.

Security alarms began to wail throughout the bank and surrounding streets. Myra and Caleb, trembling with fear, squeezed through the gash in the wall and scrambled over the rubble outside. They fled as fast as their legs could carry them past the astonished SODs. Zigzagging their way through alleys and shortcuts back towards Caleb's house, they became aware of the sound of thundering hooves, clattering through the streets behind them.

Security guards now swarmed around the bank. The police had arrived and examined the hole in the cash-machine wall, before speeding off in their cars to chase down Wooten-Maxwell and his gang.

From his office, Measles had witnessed the whole escape. His smile was eerily calm as he turned off the CCTV monitors, plunging the room into darkness. Swiftly he pulled on his long black-leather coat and swept out of the room.

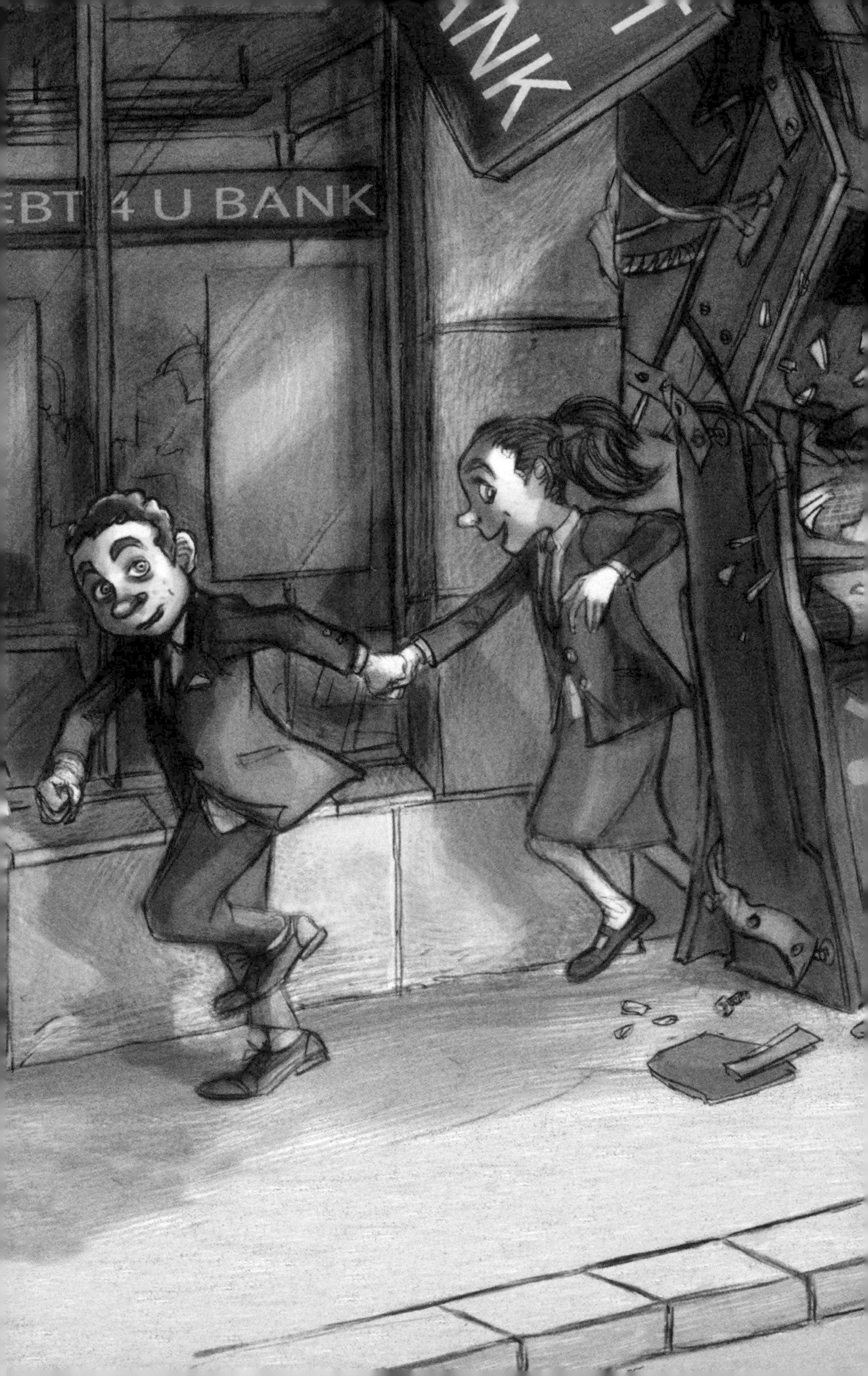
EBT 4 U BANK
NK

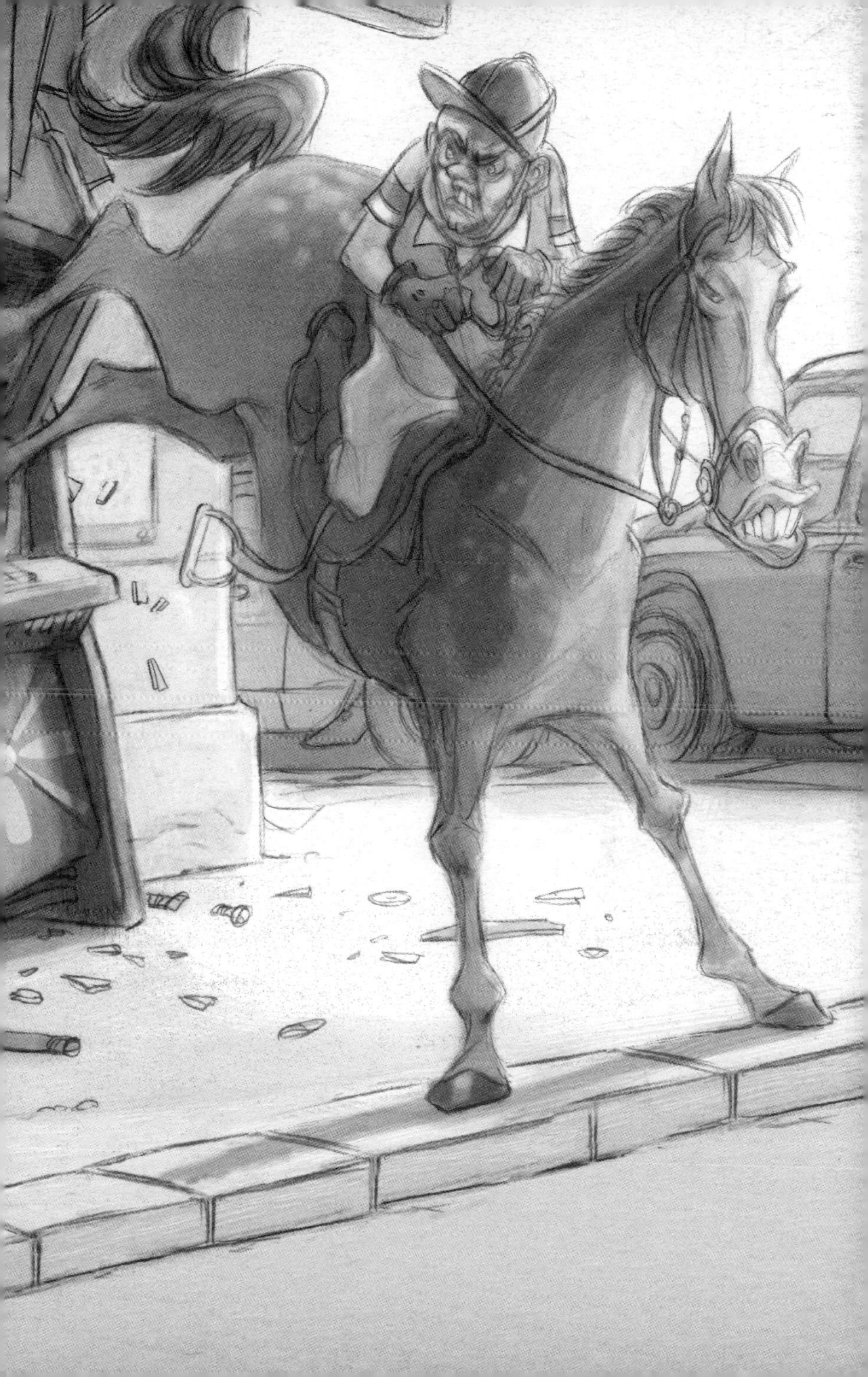

Chapter Fourteen

Police sirens continued to wail as Caleb and Myra approached the Dallaway house. They had lost Wooten-Maxwell's horse-mounted gang and had not stopped running until now. They slammed the gate behind them and ducked behind the privet hedge, gasping for breath. Squatting on the front lawn, they strained their necks towards the light coming from the lounge window. They were met with the most curious sight.

"Who's that?" asked Myra, nodding towards the house.

Caleb grinned. He could clearly see Madame Zis sitting at the table and Mopsy sitting opposite her, wearing one of her gloopy blue-cheese-and-avocado face masks. She was pushing Madame Zis's head down rather forcefully towards the tabletop. Also on the table were a bottle of sherry and two crystal glasses, both filled – and, next to them, the famous face-press.

"Go on, try it! It doesn't hurt, I promise. Here, have another sniff of sherry – *Dutch courage!*"

Madame Zis took the sherry and tossed it down her throat. Then she flopped forward onto the open plate of the face-press. "Go on zen! Get on wiz it before I change my mind!"

Caleb heard her cry of surprise as the press was clamped

shut and steam filled the room. Beside her Mopsy twittered words of encouragement. "That's it – a few seconds more – it'll be worth it, you'll see!"

Caleb heard the "ping" of the machine and saw Madame Zis sit up, her face aglow and her usually neat hair displaced and frizzy looking.

"Why, it's taken years off you, dear!" trilled Mopsy. "You hardly look old at all. It's *so* much better – take a look, won't you?"

Mopsy thrust a mirror at Madame Zis, who, on seeing her reflection, cried out again.

Outside crouched in the bushes, Myra chuckled. "I see Mopsy's the same as ever. What *is* that they're squashing their heads in?"

Caleb didn't answer. Instead he said urgently, "Let's go in. We have no time to lose."

They snuck round to the kitchen door at the back of the house and let themselves in. Caleb called out to his mother, "Mopsy! It's me, Caleb. Draw the curtains! The lounge is like a goldfish bowl. People outside can see everything you're up to!"

"Shht, shht!" he heard Mopsy hiss. "Did you hear that?"

"It zounded like zat boy!" Madame Zis said.

"It *is* me," said Caleb. "I've got out and we have to go. There's no time to explain. Just draw the curtains, will you? They'll be looking for us."

There was the sound of giggling and curtain rings being dragged along their poles. Then Mopsy came shuffling out into the hallway in her high-heeled slippers. She had clearly drunk several sherries during the course of the evening.

"CALEB!" she cried, her voice piercing his ears. She threw her arms around him and started sobbing. "Oh, Caleb, it's you – it's really you! And look who's here as well!" she gasped, catching sight of Myra. She grabbed Caleb's arm and began to dance some sort of polka, but he resisted, planting his feet firmly on the ground.

"Mum," he said, "we have to go. I know where Dad is, and we have to go and save him. Madame Zis will help us. You can't imagine how I've—"

"Madame Zis? Who's Madame Zis?"

Caleb gestured impatiently in the direction of the lounge where Madame Zis was still sitting.

"You mean *Odette*? Oh, Caleb, isn't she wonderful? And that lovely accent of hers... We've been getting on famously. She's not scary at all! She told me she comes from a different place where history got muddled or something. Or maybe it's me getting muddled. You know me and history... Anyhow she said you'd be back and that we'd go and get Bert, who's in a bit of bother, is that right?"

"He's on death row, Mum! Wanted for murder!"

"Whose murder? How absurd!"

"Madame Zis's murder... I'll explain it later. Just get her and come with me!"

Just then Madame Zis came out of the lounge and swiped at Caleb's right ear with her hand. "Where have you been, inzolent boy! You promized you'd be back and it'z been weeks! Your mozer almost had me fumigated!"

"Fumigated?" repeated Caleb, rubbing his smarting ear.

"I thought she was a *fox*..." Mopsy explained. "And, anyway, why didn't you write back, you bad boy? You know, I've been sitting here waiting for the post every day!"

"I'll explain everything – but we have to go *now*," Caleb pressed, raising his voice. "Quick, everyone in the cab..."

He ushered his mother, Madame Zis and Myra downstairs towards the garage.

"Myra, get in the back with Mum and Madame Zis. "This drive can be a bit hairy in the front…"

"Madame Zis? Who iz zis Madame Zis?" asked Madame Zis. "Why do you keep saying zat?"

"It's *you!*" Caleb answered, checking his rear-view mirror to make sure everyone was strapped in.

"Zat's not my name … my name iz—"

But Caleb wasn't listening. He leapt out of the car, opened the garage door and ran back to the car again.

Madame Zis was tapping her book, which had been left on the back seat of the cab. "It sayz it here, quite clearly, *Odette Ocelot*…"

"She's a writer, Caleb," added Mopsy. "Isn't that just so clever!"

Caleb put his foot down hard on the accelerator pedal and reversed out of the garage. "Hold on, everyone!" he said through gritted teeth.

Chapter Fifteen

It was a short drive to the airfield where Caleb hoped to make the "leap". He wound his way through the familiar back streets, Myra, Mopsy and Madame Zis sliding to and fro across the back seat like a human pendulum. But just as he approached the outskirts of town, Wooten-Maxwell galloped out across the road on his maniac horse, followed by a dozen or so mounted police in hot pursuit. Caleb swerved instinctively. Then it happened – the cab made the switch. All three in the back seat screamed with terror. A few moments later they were rocketed into Franzingland where the cab landed with a jolt.

There was pandemonium in the car. Myra was swearing. Mopsy was screaming blue murder and Madame Zis was joyfully pronouncing herself home.

Caleb hurriedly put the cab in gear and made his way towards the town hall where his father was being held captive.

"But, Caleb, where *are* we?" shrieked Mopsy. She was trembling, her hands gripping the back of Caleb's seat. Her face mask was badly smudged and clumps of avocado and blue cheese stuck to her hair.

"It's a place called Franzingland. A sort of freak glitch in history," gabbled Caleb. He knew he was pushing the cab to its limits.

"Dad got stuck here when the cab went haywire and switched without him. Right now he's on trial for the murder of Madame Zis, who was in the cab with him when the accident happened. She got stranded in Fetherham with no way of getting back and people here thought she was dead. We've got to present her to the authorities – it's the only way to get Dad off the hook."

Pulling up by the town hall they were greeted by the ominous sound of beating drums. Panels of black flags had been hoisted all along the front of the building.

"*Zut!* Zis iz not good!" exclaimed Madame Zis. "Ze beheading iz imminent – we must hurry!"

"Beheading?!" screamed Mopsy. "No one said anything to me about a BEHEADING!"

Caleb leapt from the car and pulled Madame Zis from the back seat. Myra bustled out behind her. The beating of the drums intensified as they burst through the main doors and into the foyer. A scaffold had been erected in the building's internal courtyard. There were dignitaries dressed in black robes and men in ceremonial costume solemnly milling around, waiting for the proceedings to commence. On the platform stood a simple structure comprising a vertical frame supporting a wide blade suspended from a pulley. At the base of the frame was a horizontal plank fitted with leather straps. A scooped out chopping block was positioned under the blade and beneath that a simply woven basket was placed on the ground. A bulky man in a black hood was checking the mechanism over.

"Identity, please," said the man behind the front desk.

Caleb pushed Madame Zis in front of him. "It's her, she's alive – Odette Ocelot. There's been a big mistake. YOU MUST CALL OFF THE EXECUTION!"

Madame Zis smoothed her hair and straightened her shoulders, ready for inspection. Just then Mopsy, who had been left in the car on her own, crashed angrily in through the doors and, on seeing the scaffold, began to yell again.

"Stop screaming, Mother!" bellowed Caleb.

Mopsy looked desperately from Caleb to Madame Zis. "Somebody do something!" she gulped.

The drums beat louder and louder.

"*Enter ze Templar Bourdonzac Regiment...*" boomed a voice from the loudspeaker.

A parade of uniformed guards marched onto the platform and took their places around the guillotine. They were dressed in chainmail, over which they wore white tunics bearing Celtic-style red crosses. Each carried a "bourdonzac", an instrument similar to the one played by the busker outside the Fezerham library. Once the regiment was in place, the loudspeaker boomed out again: "*Bring in ze condemned...*"

The drums ceased their foreboding beating and began a military *rattata-rattata-tat*. The guards put their instruments to their lips and began to play. The piece was weighty and morose, fitting the occasion perfectly, and the effect of the amassed bourdonzacs was deafening.

The man behind the desk raised his voice above the din of the pipes. "I need identification, please." He held out his hand for their papers. "I cannot let you in without it!"

Caleb thrust Madame Zis's book towards him. With trembling hands he opened it to the page bearing her picture. "It's her! It's her!" Then he held the page next to Madame Zis's face so the official could appreciate the likeness. The man grimaced and cupped his hand behind his ear, struggling to hear.

"She's *alive*!" shouted Caleb. "They are going to execute my dad – but it's *her*, don't you see? THERE'S GOING TO BE A GROSS MISCARRIAGE OF JUSTICE – WE MUST STOP IT!"

The man behind the desk looked slowly between the photo and Madame Zis. "She looks razer younger zan in zis photo..." he mused, peering closely at the book.

"Ha ha! That'll be the face-press!" piped up Mopsy. "I told you it works wonders!"

Just then a tall, imposing man with a square chin and solemn expression entered the foyer. He was dressed in full regalia, including a fur-trimmed velvet cloak. Around his waist hung a long sword, its hilt studded with jewels, and in his right hand he carried a ceremonial shield, which

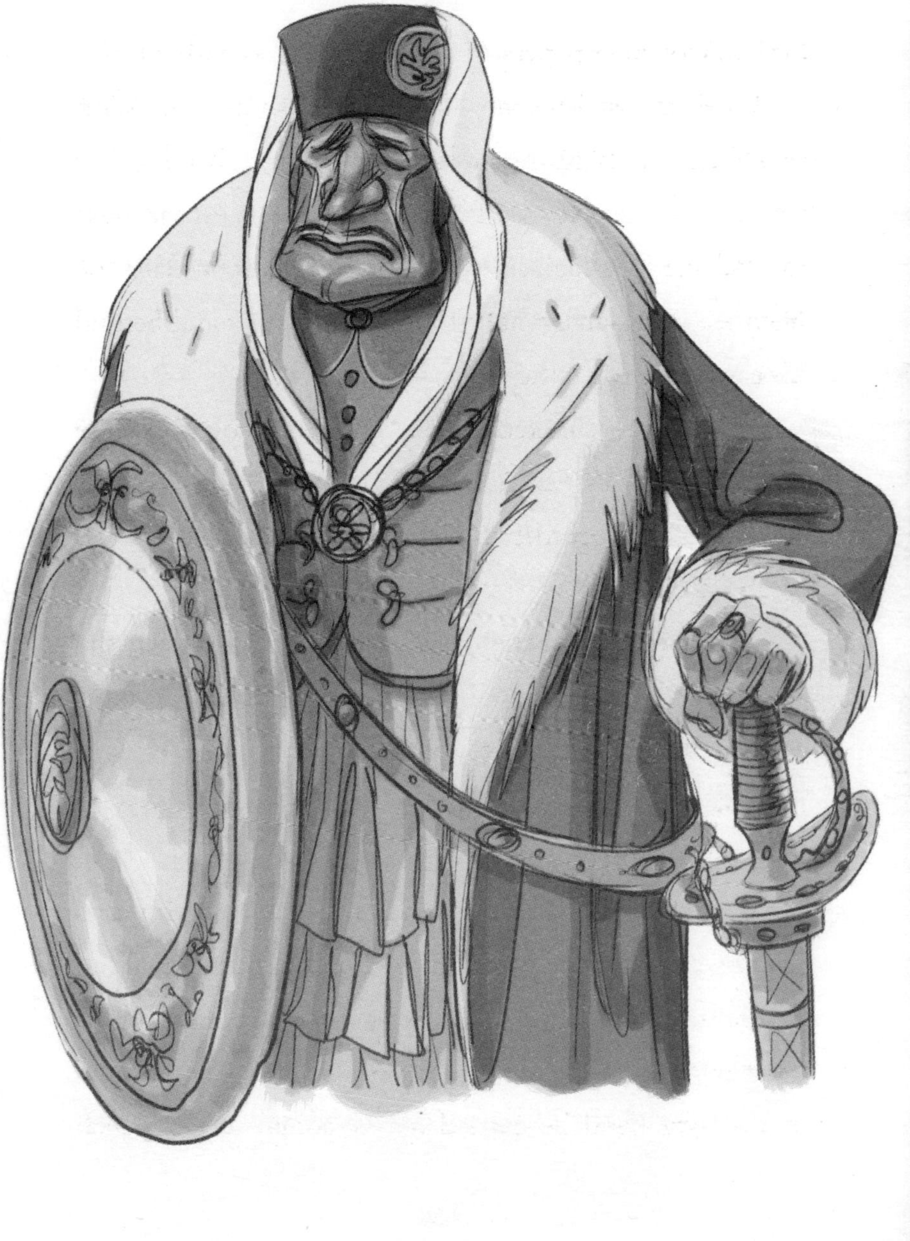

was so large it covered most of his torso. He wore a bulky medallion round his neck and metal boots that jingled as he walked. In his presence, Mme Zis came over all decorous and sombre. As he swept past them, in his fur trimmed velvet cloak she lowered her eyes and bobbed her knees in a curtsy in a formal act of reverence.

"Who's that?" hissed Caleb, pulling at her sleeve.

"Monsieur ze Grand Master, of course!" She looked shocked at Caleb's ignorance. "He will prezide over ze proceedings…"

Caleb watched as the Grand Master made his way up the stone steps behind the front desk. A sign at the foot of the stairs read Law Lords' Gallery, First Floor and bore an arrow pointing upwards.

"I'm afraid I need legitimate proof of identity for zis woman – zis iz not sufficient," bawled the official, indicating Madame Zis's book.

"But it's all we have!" cried Caleb, desperately.

The man behind the desk gave a shrug, a gesture that declared deadlock.

Caleb grabbed Madame Zis's hand and made a dash

for the stairs. "Cover me, Myra!" he called out as he spun Madame Zis round on her heels and sped away in pursuit of the Grand Master.

As the official fumbled for his panic button, Myra leapt forward and grabbed his ears with both hands. She pulled him face-down onto his desk, disabling him instantly. The man let out a howl of pain.

Caleb sprung up the wide stone steps two at a time, dragging Madame Zis behind him. The Law Lords' Gallery was an open arcade spanning the width of the courtyard. There was a bird's-eye view of the execution platform. Two armed guards stood at the entrance.

"I must speak to the Grand Master!" gasped Caleb.

The guards remained rigid and unresponsive.

Caleb stood on the tips of his toes, trying to see past them. He could just make out three very old men in black robes, each with a square of black cloth on their head – a sign of their unanimous decision that the execution should proceed. The Grand Master had taken his seat at their right. He had put his shield down and was checking a pocket-watch while wiping his nose with his handkerchief.

He sighed, slumped back in his chair and plonked his metal-booted feet up on a small stool.

Bert was led onto the platform. Caleb's heart sank. He was almost beyond recognition – a shadow of the man Caleb loved so much. He looked bedraggled and frail, wearing a stubbly beard and saggy clothes with his hands cuffed together in shackles. Caleb felt a painful lump rise in his throat. It hurt horribly to see his feisty, strong father so doleful. He swallowed hard and fought against a debilitating sense of dread. Meanwhile a man in a black bowler hat made Bert lie face down before strapping him to the guillotine's plank.

"That man down there," Caleb yelled at the guards, "he's *innocent*! The woman he is supposed to have murdered is here with me – look! She's alive!" He jiggled Madame Zis's arm aloft like she was a puppet on a string.

The guards remained impassive.

"Let me through to the gallery," pleaded Caleb. "I must speak to the Grand Master. This man is innocent and he'll *die* if you don't!"

The guards raised their shields to block his way. It was useless negotiating. Without a moment's thought, he shoved Madame Zis towards them like a human battering ram. They caught her, staggering backwards with surprise. As she yelped in indignation, Caleb leapt onto the gallery parapet and hurled himself at a nearby rope, suspended from a flagpole. The rope swung out across the courtyard. Some of the Templar Bourdonzac Regiment dived to the ground to avoid being struck as he swooped inches from their heads. Others, not so quick, found themselves kicked down like tenpins by his swinging feet. The bourdonzacs buzzed and farted like giant deflating balloons as the players toppled and the music came to a halt.

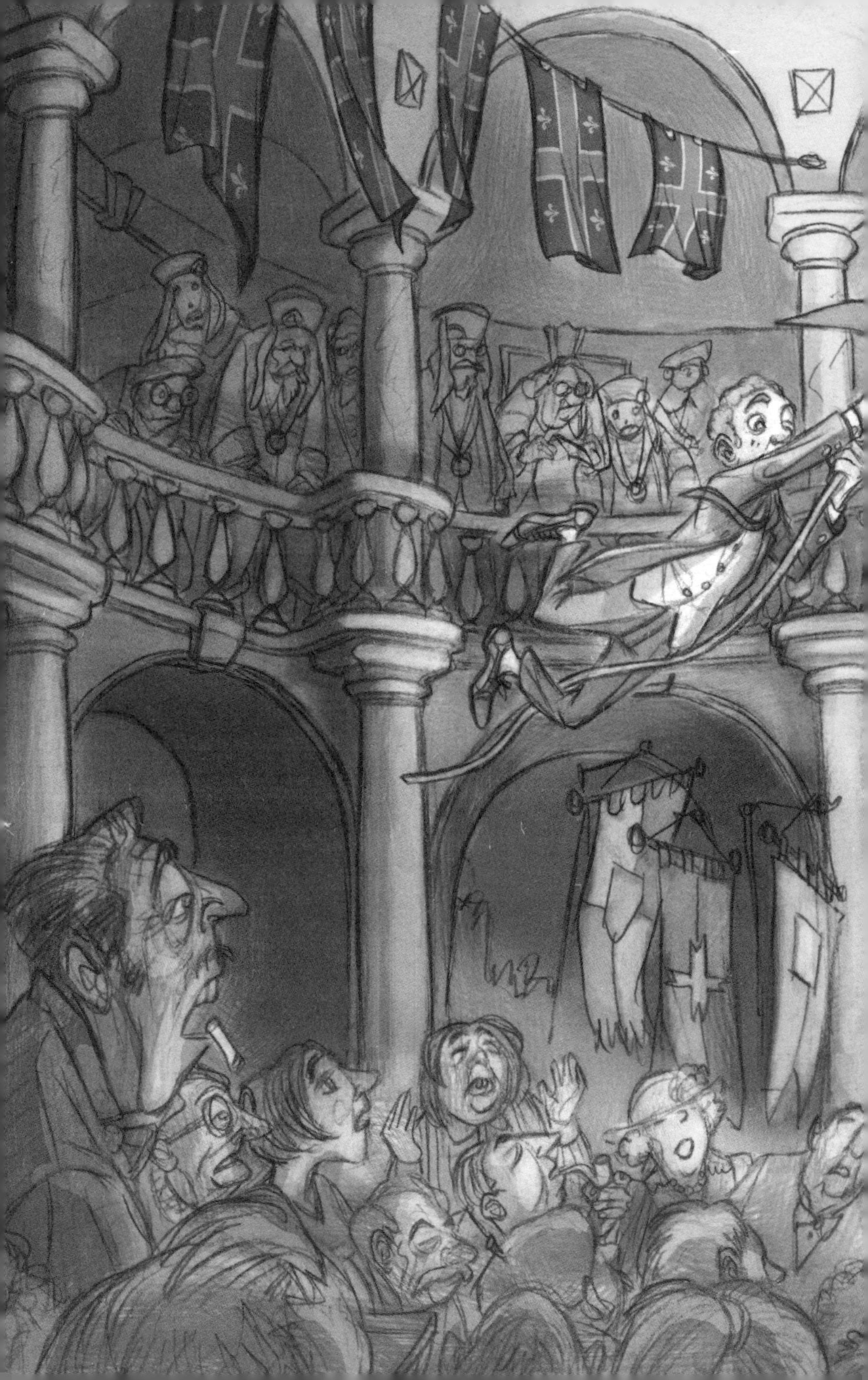

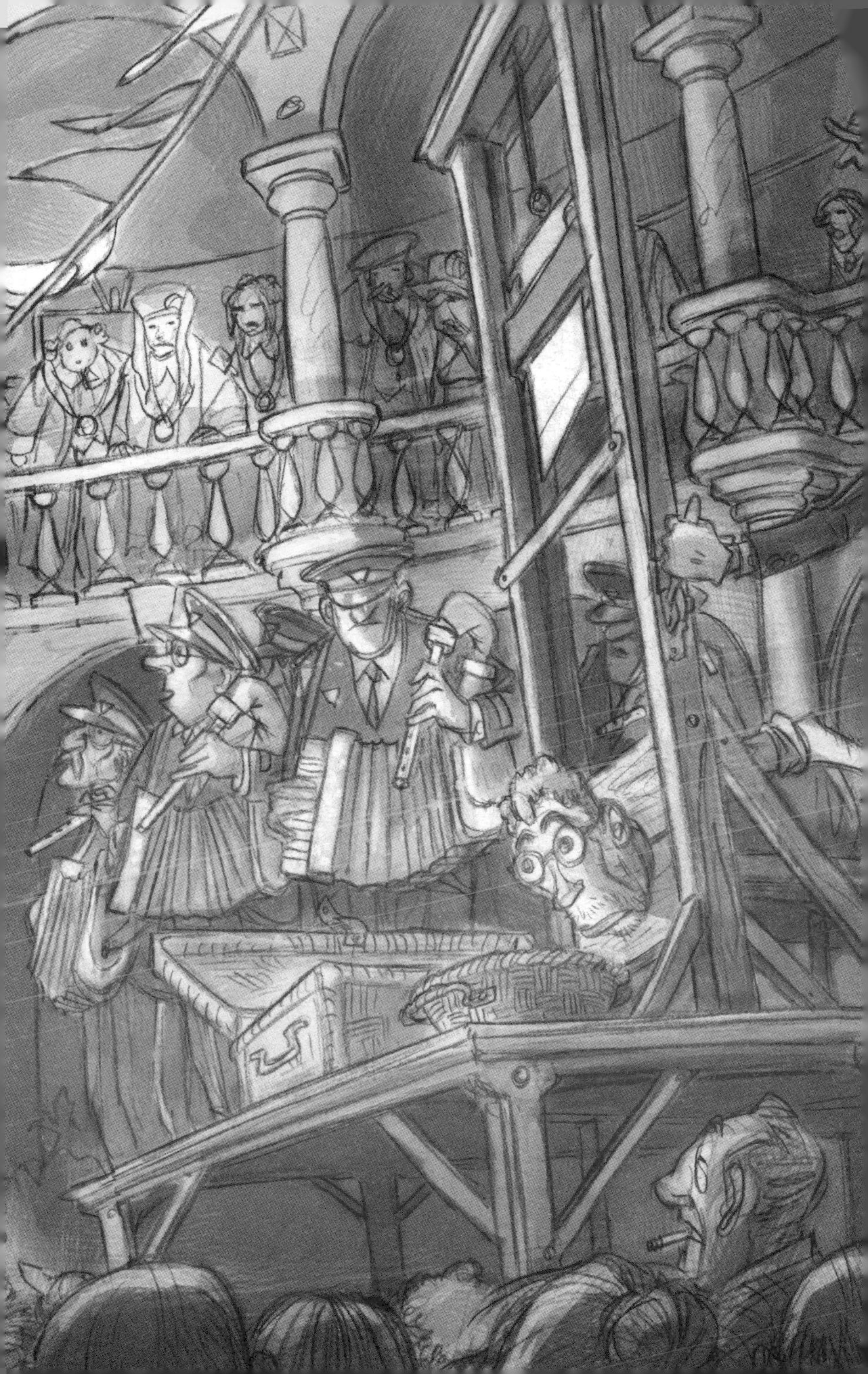

Having swung the full width of the courtyard, Caleb changed trajectory to return over the scaffold. His hands slipped and burned on the coarse rope causing him to cry out in terror and rage. His grip on the rope loosened and he let go, crashing headlong into the guillotine apparatus. The impact caused the bascule plank to snap forward and before he knew it, Caleb heard the swish of the blade as it whistled downwards and landed with a heavy *thwunk*.

After a few moments of silence, mutters of confusion began to reverberate throughout the courtyard. Caleb sat rigid in the tangled woodwork of the collapsed guillotine, his eyes squeezed shut and his bile rising in dread. He opened one eye, then the other, and was met by the sight of his father's head on the platform, inches from his feet.

"Caleb?" the head inquired, its glassy eyes peering up at him curiously.

Caleb's wits failed him and the courtyard began to spin uncontrollably. With a giddy surge, the faces of the puzzled, whispering crowd whirled around and around, over and over. The blood drained from Caleb's face and he fell into a dead faint, crashing down onto the platform next to his father's body.

Chapter Sixteen

Caleb was brought round by the sensation of cold water splashing onto his face. A cacophony of voices babbled above his head.

"Iz zere blood?" one asked. "Waz he hit by ze blade?"

"No – he'z just fainted, ze poor boy. He had ze fright of hiz life…"

"He'z been passed out for quite a while – should we call ze ambulance?"

Caleb opened his eyes. Strong arms supported him as he tried to sit up.

"Heh! Voilà! Make some space, everyone. He iz back among us."

Madame Zis's concerned face peered over him. "Caleb! Oh, you ridiculous boy, what were you zinking? You could have killed yourself!"

Caleb rubbed his eyes. "But instead I killed Dad," he mumbled miserably.

"No! I'm here, Caleb," said Bert. He was crouched next to Caleb, crying but smiling at the same time. Astonishingly he was back in one piece. "That was quite the stunt you pulled off there, son!"

Caleb gasped. He jumped up and pulled his father to his feet, throwing his arms around his still bound body. He buried his face in his father's shirt, breathing in his familiar biscuity smell.

"Untie me?" Bert ventured gently.

Caleb hurriedly undid the ropes so Bert could finally take him in his arms.

"Oh, my Caleb! My beautiful, clever, crazy boy..."

"I thought I'd killed you!" gasped Caleb.

Bert kissed the side of Caleb's head and clasped him tightly. Behind him Caleb saw the rope on which he had swung dangling limply above the collapsed frame of the guillotine.

"Ze impact of you crashing into the guillotine dislodged ze blade from ze crossbar," explained the executioner, gruffly.

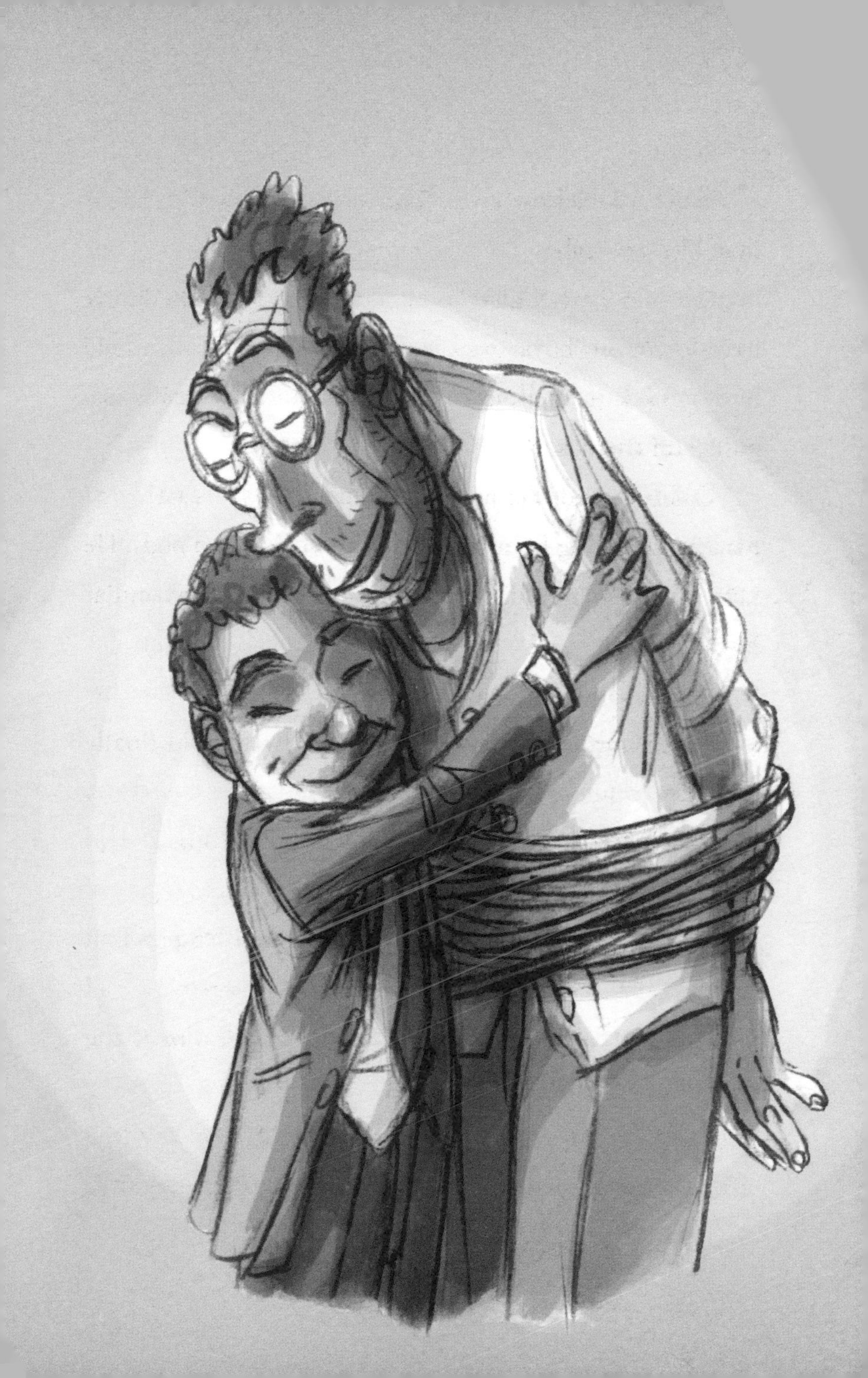

"Ze blade was released but waz in freefall. It missed your fazer's head by centimetres! Zis model iz an antique! It iz part of our heritage and you have reduced it to splinterz!" He was clearly none too pleased. The thick blade was now deeply embedded in the wooden platform, uncomfortably close to where Caleb sat. It still quivered to and fro from the force of the impact.

"Your fazer's body was trapped under ze structure. Zat iz why you only saw hiz head!" Madame Zis added with a smile.

A figure appeared, its shadow looming over them.

"Caleb, zis iz ze Grand Master," continued Madame Zis. "My sister iz here, my daughter too – zey have confirmed my identification..." There were tears of joy in her eyes.

Just then merry chaos broke out across the courtyard. On the Grand Master's signal, the Law Lords had laid down the squares of black cloth from their heads. A stay of execution was proclaimed and there was heartfelt relief all round as Bert was pronounced a free man.

Back in the foyer, Mopsy had succeeded in distracting the policemen who were attempting to arrest Myra by feigning a seizure. As they sprung to resuscitate her, the official behind the desk rang for an ambulance. It was only when Caleb walked back into the entrance hall with his father that Mopsy ceased her swooning and gagging and ran to her husband, throwing herself around his neck.

"Bertie, oh, Bertie – I'm so glad you're safe. Tell me everything will be all right now? You can't imagine how I've struggled without you..." She clutched at his hair and clung to him with all her might, leaving blobs of her face mask in his stubble.

Caleb ran to Myra. "Are you OK?" he asked, embracing her.

She nodded, smiling.

"Is *she* OK?" the official behind the desk grumbled. "She damn near ripped my earz off!"

Just then, Madame Zis joined them in the foyer. She was flushed and happy, and followed by her friends and family. "Zank you, Caleb," she said, squeezing his arm.

"Thank YOU," he replied, and leaned in to give her a quick peck on her papery-skinned cheek.

She blushed with pleasure. "You are a *good* boy," she said.

There was a pause. "Well," Caleb ventured. "I suppose this is goodbye."

"Yes, it must be zis way. We should never have met in ze first place now, should we?" she said, winking at him.

They shook hands, and Caleb, Myra, Mopsy and Bert, smiling left the town hall.

Once outside, they hugged again. Bert stood tall, pushing back his shoulders and breathing in the sweet air of freedom.

"Shall we go home, Dad?" asked Caleb, slipping his hand into his father's.

"Nothing would make me happier," said Bert, squeezing hard. "After you, son…"

Caleb stepped onto the pavement in front of the town hall and looked up and down the street. There was no sign of the cab anywhere! Puzzled, he scratched his head. He was sure of where he had left it but, at the same time, he doubted his senses as he gazed at the empty space where the car should have been parked. He turned to Myra. "It was here, right?"

She nodded in confirmation.

"The wretched cab must have gone awol again," said Bert, scratching his head.

"Well, find it at once!" exclaimed Mopsy. "We're

trapped here without it!"

Just then, something on the ground caught Myra's eye. She bent and picked it up. "Caleb, look!" she said, holding out a flat object. It was the same size and shape as a credit card, with a series of squiggles, dots and lines on it.

Caleb stared at it in horror.

"What is it?" cried Mopsy, seeing the expression on his face.

Caleb took the object from Myra and turned it around in his fingers in dismal recognition.

"I've never seen anything like it before..." whispered Myra.

"I have," replied Caleb grimly. "It's called a DNA profile. This is Measles's identity badge. He followed us here..."

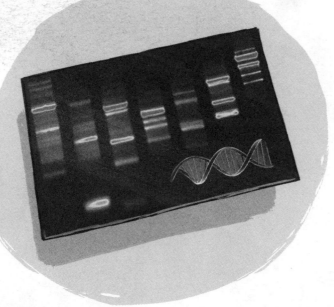

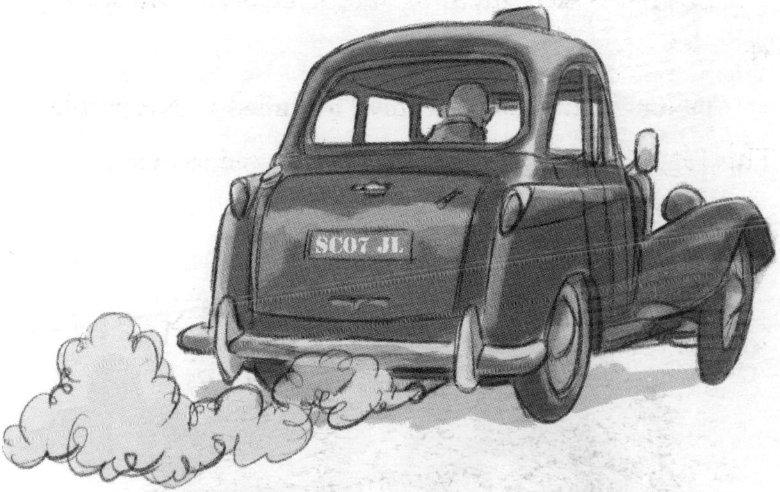
SC07 JL

TO BE CONTINUED...

Sally Chomet is a writer with a professional background in both public relations and film production, working closely with Sylvain on *Belleville Rendez-Vous* and *The Illusionist*. Since then Sally has been writing full-time whilst providing language services in both translation and teaching fields. *Caleb's Cab* will be her first published work. Sally (British) and Sylvain (French) met in Toronto, have been married since 2000 and live with their two young children in the South of France.

Sylvain Chomet is a world-class film director and Bafta and César award winner. He also has multiple Oscar nominations to his name for his animated films *Belleville Rendez-Vous* (2004) and *The Illusionist* (2011). In 2013 Sylvain released, to critical acclaim, a live-action feature called *Attila Marcel* which he wrote and directed. He has also guest directed a 'couch gag' spot for *The Simpsons* and an animated music video for Belgian pop superstar Stromae.

CREDIT · PHOTO BY
Christophe
BOUQUET